1-78

Grave of Green Water

by Jan Roffman

GRAVE OF GREEN WATER
ASHES IN AN URN
A PENNY FOR THE GUY
DEATH OF A FOX
WITH MURDER IN MIND

Grave of
Green Water

Jan Roffman

1968
Published for the Crime Club by
Doubleday & Company, Inc.
Garden City, New York

All of the characters in this book
are fictitious, and any resemblance
to actual persons, living or dead,
is purely coincidental.

Grave of Green Water

Chapter 1

Though Mrs Wisley was a sturdy body, teetering on the rim of middle-age, with a thumping step that rattled the loose panes of the glass pen behind the motor showroom that served Ashley Jones as an office, he behaved as if she were invisible. With brow sculpted into lines, mouth lightly pursed, fingers absently ranging through a file, he presented for her edification an executive so deeply committed to his job that he could not subtract a second to acknowledge her presence.

Since in theory—though not in practice—he'd been her boss for two years, his little charade was wasted, it being Mildred Wisley's contention that Ashley Jones was incapable of honest toil. Conceited, downright dishonest, eye ever pricked for the main chance . . . she could have gone on counting his sins till kingdom come, hate for him a never-healing blister on her heart.

She thrust a clipped sheaf of papers under his nose. "Daily reports, Mr Jones. It's gone half-past five. I'm off."

Without lingering for his nod of dismissal, she made for her own glass-paned door. Vanessa, the "child" whose ability to type was nullified by the fact that she couldn't spell, so was useless except for making tea, doing the filing, had bolted while Mrs Wisley's back was turned. Since it was a daily occurrence it caused her no surprise.

She grasped the carrier bag of shopping bought in her lunch hour, straightened the lapels of her navy and white foulard, and without so much as a glance at hair or face— both were set to rights at 8.30 A.M. and expected to last the day out—left with just nice time to catch her Helton bus.

She called good night to old Sam Goodsell who except on Wednesdays took over the pumps from 5.30 to 11. He was sixty-two, lame in one leg, none too nippy with change, but, since in his youth he'd been a member of the Old Man's cricket team, he was privileged. Folks said hard things about Frederick Gasson, they always had, but no one could accuse him of disloyalty to the pals of his youth.

To reach the bus stop she had to circle the half-acre of second-hand cars. They seemed to her to breed in the night. Some of them had been out, rain and shine, for over a year. No blinking the fact that thanks to Mr Ashley Jones the business was skidding downhill. She'd have found herself a new job months ago, only Mr Gasson had begged her to stay, sworn she was the only member of his staff he could trust, which she could well believe! Minus her and Mr West, who managed the caravan sales, Gasson's Garage and Car Salerooms would have been lost in the red by now. Of course, everyone knew the Old Man didn't need the money. But the Crumley garage had given him his start and, as long as he'd been able, he'd run it himself. To see it overtaken by upstart competitors must be murder for him.

At such moments Mrs Wisley's imagination was apt to throw up pictures of devils armed with toasting forks, prison cells where warders thrust crusts of bread and tin mugs of water through a hatch in the door, even gibbets. Though they didn't hang people any longer; and more the pity. Ashley Jones had earned that fate long before his shifty blue eyes had picked out Meg Gasson to keep him in idleness for life.

She sighed as she often did for the cruel fate that had overtaken Frederick Gasson in his fifties: two felling blows that would have finished most men. The crash in a private plane belonging to a friend that had smashed his spine, the marriage of his only child to a handsome ne'er-do-well, who treated the petty cash as if it were his own pocket money.

For five minutes after he'd heard the old bag leave, Ashley turned a blind eye to the clip of papers. No point in studying them. Whether they were good or bad, they would call forth no variation of response in the man for whom they'd been prepared. If the day had included the sale of three Rolls-Royces, the Red Man would only have grunted, assumed his son-in-law had pulled off a shady deal with a gang of crooks.

When, at last, he condescended to flick them over, he learned from the typed columns set for comparison against last year's takings that the continuing heat wave had maintained the petrol and sundries sales high, that receipts for repairs and servicing were down. Car sales nil. But, ha, trust teacher's pet, Tony West had bamboozled some innocent into signing on the dotted line for a caravan. Ashley folded the sheets to fit the breast pocket of his hand-tailored linen jacket. After two years' practice, he made a neat job of it.

That done, he twisted round to gaze at himself in the twelve-inch square of mirror suspended from a nail on the partition, stroke his blond hair that was neither thinning nor fading, while congratulating himself upon a facial bone structure that gave nose, forehead and jawline near-classical perfection. His mid-blue eyes were protected by dark lashes as long as a girl's, smooth, unstained lids. Not a blemish on his skin. Teeth perfect. In all honesty he could not detect the faintest sign of deterioration. For further confirmation he tried out three separate smiles: whimsical, grave, enticing. Finally, he switched on his masterpiece: his cherishing smile against which no woman was proof. Even the Red Man hadn't been able to filch his most valuable asset: looks that were instantly arresting, not lightly forgotten.

He locked up, checked that the door to the Stores was padlocked, ran his eye down the yard to make sure the shutter was clamped down over the workshop. It was. Trust those guys to be away like greased lightning by 5.30. Nodding to old Goodsell, he speculated idly on how much he managed to fiddle out of the petrol till, then strolled with the man-of-the-world gait he'd perfected in his teens to the parking dock where the Jag was protected from the vehicles of female customers who were unreliable in reverse. Reaching it, he slotted key into lock with a glow of possession that was within touching distance of love. At least he'd squeezed her out of the Red Man.

As he waited to cross the stream of traffic he automatically subsided into the fantasy in which he indulged himself five evenings a week. Instead of cruising at forty for three-quarters of a mile, he put his foot down, flew past the gates of Laburnum Lodge, hell-bent for the nearest Channel port, on to the car ferry, off into Europe, burrowing deeper and deeper south, a man who was master of his days, not office lackey to a hulking megalomaniac by the name of Frederick Gasson.

He *could* do it. That was the grit that gave the dream substance. He had the tools. Inside a locked drawer in his office desk, the key of which never left his person, was a deed box. It contained one hundred pound notes, a passport he'd been at pains to acquire a month after his wedding day.

But the bill rendered for freedom would be a high one. When the Red Man kicked the bucket and willed his only child, his all, Meg, under loving persuasion could be counted on to allow him to turn the bulk into cash, invest or spend it as he fancied. But if he bolted while the Red Man was alive, there was no absolute surety that Meg, lovesick as she was, would take him back to her bosom, share the spoils. There were occasions when Meg was capable of astonishing—and frustrating—him. He thought, with no apprehension at being present when it came about, that by the time she reached middle-age, Meg would be as pig-headed and obtuse as her dad.

He changed down, flicked out his indicator, and for comfort wrapped himself around in the alternative dream.

How long, after the Red Man was underground, would they have to wait to lay their hands on the cash, move out of Crumley? In addition to Gasson's Garage and Car Salerooms, there were share holdings, substantial blocks of property, land in Helton to realise. A few discreet enquiries had led him to arrive at an estimate of six months. Then! He contemplated the choice before him like a hungry man examining the menu of a four-star hotel. A restaurant-bar on the Costa Brava? The West Indies? Tangier? Sun, cheap labour, a patron in a white dinner jacket whose most onerous task would be to exert authority, rain smiles on favoured customers, suffer the fawning attention of unescorted females. The idyllic prospect ahead rubbed another hole in his patience; soon . . . it had got to be soon.

On entering the conventionally styled brick villa the Red Man had built himself in the thirties when he'd first found himself touching prosperity, he actually gritted his teeth. Fifteen minutes if he were lucky, twenty at the worst, and his daily dose of gall would be swallowed. Brace yourself, boy, he whispered. He can't kill you, though, by God, he'd like to.

Inside the hall he called his wife's name. It never did any harm to get advance information on the state of the Red Man's temper: bad or diabolical.

A reply came from the room leading off to the left. "That you, Ashley? Come on in. Meg's out."

Ashley had never seen Frederick Gasson on his feet. He prayed he never would. The sentence of crippling immobility had already been pronounced when Meg, holding his hand, had led him into the newly erected ground-floor suite in which Frederick Gasson appeared doomed to spend the remainder of his days on earth. Then, as now, Hexham, the male-nurse, had been in attendance, a creep in a white coat. Meg had announced in a stiff, little-girl voice: "Daddy, this is Ashley. You remember I told you all about him."

Hexham, again as now, was dismissed by a gesture to his adjoining quarters, thus restricting his sight and hearing to the dimension of the key-hole.

On sight Ashley had re-christened Frederick Gasson the Red Man: lumpily fleshy face the colour of an unripe tomato, bald pink skull caught here and there with tufts of mahogany hair, an instantaneously combustible temper.

He'd primed himself sufficiently on his prospective father-in-law not to be caught wrong-footed by the malevolence beamed upon him out of slit-eyes so narrow it was impossible to name their colour.

"Aye, you told me."

Determinedly Meg had pulled Ashley closer to the bed made mountainous by Frederick Gasson's belly. "Daddy, we are going to be married. We're in love, and Daddy, I am twenty-six . . ."

"Free by law to marry any man you choose! You don't have to remind me. You've said it often enough."

A life under Frederick Gasson's roof had taught Meg the trick of handling him: refuse to play temper against temper. Never argue, but make short, unequivocal statements, a course made easier by the fact that she was devoted to him.

"Daddy, we want your blessing. You know that perfectly well, so don't pretend you don't. And we want to live with you. It would be a perfect solution: me running the house, Ashley managing the business . . . of course under your direction."

"What's he know about it?"

"I've explained. He's an experienced car salesman. He was one once in London. He's never actually managed a garage, but if you'll teach him, he'll soon learn." She'd pressed Ashley's hand, imperceptibly drawn back, leaving him to go on from there, confident that she couldn't lose. And she hadn't. Both of them bankrupt, one in money, the other in mobility, it had been a foregone conclusion that she would coerce them into a bargain sealed with worm and gallwood.

Even allowing for Ashley's prejudice, Frederick Gasson was physically unattractive. His manner and speech were graceless for the reason he'd never found time nor inclination to sweeten them. Now, labouring under intolerable frustration, doggedly riding out the black days when he wished he was dead, he growled more often than he spoke. He did so now. "Come on, come on. Where's the day's figures?"

Hiding his revulsion for the outstretched pudgy hand, the lard-white skin of which sprouted red, wire-stiff hairs, Ashley obeyed. With a flick of his eye he noticed that the door of the adjoining bathroom was unobtrusively ajar providing a wider space for Hexham's snooping ear. Slave-boy with a white skin. Roger Hexham! A spasm of memory threw back at him one of the Red Man's first taunts: "Ashley! What sort of a name do you call that!"

If he'd replied that his mother had read *Gone With the Wind* during her pregnancy, the Red Man would have been no wiser, so he'd held his revenge on ice until his son was born.

Meg had wheedled: "Darling, we haven't finally decided what to call him. Of course he has to have your name, but it would be muddling to have two Ashleys, so I thought . . ." She'd paused, eyes pleading, big mouth smiling to urge her hope. "It would give Daddy such a thrill if we called him Frederick. Frederick Ashley Jones. Yes?"

Over his dead body. He'd made a play of considering the idea before he pronounced gravely: "Philip would be my choice."

"Philip!" She'd looked confounded. "But we don't know anyone called Philip."

"Not personally."

With Meg never very quick in the uptake, it had taken a moment for the significance to dawn. "I see what you mean . . . but I don't know."

Naturally, in the end, he'd won, and his son was baptised Philip Jones, nicknamed Pip, and the Red Man's dream of a grandson named after him was slugged on the head.

Frederick Gasson read every figure through twice, dropped the sheets on the bed. They were no worse than he'd anticipated, but his impotence to make an honest workman out of the handsome poppinjay Meg had wished upon him, got no easier to bear. "That the lot?"

"Yes. Where's Meg?"

"Took the boy and drove off for a picnic. Said she'd be back by half-past five." He breathed in to quell the ire that threatened to suffocate him. "It's twelve weeks since you made a car sale. What do you do with yourself all day?"

"See potential customers, run the business."

"Bah! Mrs Wisley and Tom Norris do that. You sit on your backside all day."

Without visible offence Ashley murmured: "That's a customary posture in an office, I believe. Is that all?"

"Yes. You can give West a message for me. Tell him I'd like to see him here in the morning. Ten o'clock."

Ashley spent his lowest-powered smile on the Red Man. Discounting Meg, who loyally refused to play, Frederick Gasson's army of spies in his running war against Ashley Jones numbered five: Hexham, Mrs Wisley, Tony West, Sam Goodsell and Tom Norris, the head mechanic. Their wages? The Red Man's promissory notes to fall due on the day when Ashley Jones's downfall was accomplished—which would never dawn.

At the door he called good night, spoke under his breath the two words of silent prayer he always uttered whenever he left the Red Man's presence: Drop dead. And he would too. All Ashley had to work out was how and when.

At the sight of Ashley's parked car, Meg was pitchforked into one of her all too frequent attacks of self-abasement. "Oh, dear," she wailed to her son asleep in a carry-cot on the rear seat: "Daddy's home first!"

Her afternoons were hitched to a dream: Pip lying rose-like in his pretty nursery, herself changed, every crease smoothed out of her, decanter in hand when Ashley emerged from his evening session with her father, offering him an idyll of young wifehood as compensation for the indignities forced upon him because he was not his own boss. About once a fortnight she got there. And she would have today if it hadn't been for all that fuss with the police.

An endearingly ordinary girl, thin, still a bit gangling, with mid-brown hair lapping irregular features, there was a mild note of panic in her splendid dark eyes, as she hoisted

her son out of his cot, balanced him on her hip, hurried indoors. The Gasson girl, as most people went on calling her,
had never been blessed with beauty, but she'd a sound
heart, nice ways with her, and everyone had believed a
head on her shoulders until she confounded them by marrying Ashley Jones.

She called from the hall: "Ashley . . . Ashley . . . Darling,
where are you?"

She located him on the flagged terrace outside the living-
room, a drink in his hand. She put Pip into his arms, kissed
him as passionately as if she'd lived all day with the expectation of not being reunited with him this side of the grave.
It was a supposition with a small basis of truth. Flickers of
doubt, spiders' webs of dread did plague her whenever he
was out of sight. She had grown as inured to them as to a
minor ailment, like sinus trouble or a tendency to acne. They
were the pay-off for the miracle of being Ashley Jones's wife.

There it was again, Ashley thought irritably, that production of re-presenting him with the fruit of her womb. It
happened at least once every weekday and twice on Sundays.

The desire to absolve herself sent Meg headlong into a
rush of explanation. "It was Moira's idea. A picnic, for her
two boys and Pip. She said Framley Woods, because it
would be cooler in the shade. But we ran into a road block,
so we had to turn off and go on to Haremare Common. And
then there was so much traffic coming back with the police
cordoning off the road round the reservoir that it took simply ages to get home. Darling, I'm sorry. I hate being out
when you get back. Now, I'll have to feed Pip and get him
to bed . . ." She laid her cheek shamefacedly against his.
"Supper's going to be late. Will you mind?"

He moved his head in denial. "Why were the police cordoning off the road?"

"Because they found a body . . . well, I suppose it can't be a body, more likely a skeleton by now. A woman's. There were a whole gang of them, busy as bees." She wrinkled her nose as if she smelt something nasty. "Sergeant Trent said it must have been buried before the reservoir was flooded. Some boys found it."

"Found it where?"

"In that old ruined cottage. Keeper's Cottage, I think it was called. It went under when they took the whole of Dene Valley for a reservoir. Don't you remember, they started flooding it soon after we were married?" Under the nostalgia of memory she relaxed, the upper half of her body sharing his knee with Pip, her expression released from guilt at making him wait for his supper. "Libby and I went for a walk there that spring. It made me sad to think that all those beautiful trees and fields were going to be drowned alive. There were two marvellous old farms, lots of cottages with heavenly gardens, even a roadside chapel. I know we've got to have more water, but it seemed a shame."

"What were the boys doing, skin-diving?"

She threw him a mock chiding glance. "Don't you ever read the papers? The drought has dried up over half the new reservoir. You can walk over huge areas of it now. It's all wired off, but people get under the fence, or over it. I suppose that's what the boys did. They found it inside the ruins of Keeper's Cottage, buried under rocks and stones. Almost like a proper grave, only it hadn't been dug."

"You went to look at it?"

She shook her head, made squeamish by the thought. "No one was allowed near. But Sergeant Trent, who was helping to man the road-block, had. I didn't want to listen, but Moira kept pestering him for details. She's a real ghoul."

Pip whimpered, and recognising it as a warning light,

Meg lifted him into her arms. "He's so sleepy, he'll drop off in no time. Supper won't be long."

She had reached the threshold of the sitting-room, when he turned his head, called to her: "Do they know who she was?"

"Darling, how can they pin a name on a skeleton! But Sergeant Trent said with all the scientific know-how they have nowadays, it won't be long before they do."

The sensation he underwent was not as stunning as shock: rather a wondering bemusement that the dead past could spring alive from Meg's inane chatter; that the waters could recede and expose a grave; that Keeper's Cottage should possess a supernatural power to rear itself out of the watery oblivion in which he had imagined it had sunk till Doomsday.

After a moment he stood up, descended three curved steps flanked by rose beds, and then under the still powerful beat of the sun proceeded in an arrow-straight line to the end of the parched lawn. At the base-line were four laburnum trees, their branches festooned with shrivelled pods. He turned, surveyed the two storeys of the house which the Red Man's wing made lop-sided, then after a pause, retraced his steps to the terrace.

Back in his chair he poured himself another drink, sipped half of it, then put it down with a violent jolt. Had he actually moved out of the chair, or had it been no more than an intention in his mind? He didn't know, which was proof that it had happened again, for the first time in two years, that treacherous slip of a memory-cog that stole fractions out of his life. As a boy it had scared him, but, by now, repetition had dulled its power to alarm. Until that last time the stolen minutes had never caused him serious embarrassment. Certainly no one suspected that his brain contained a minute fault that subjected him to short, wide-spaced black-outs.

Well, it assuredly didn't matter a damn whether or not he'd walked to the end of the garden.

Roughly he shrugged off the awkward reminder of the flaw in his anatomy, concentrated on sifting the few grits of hard fact from Meg's chatter.

That some woman's bones had been disinterred by a gang of prowling boys didn't necessarily mean it was the same woman. Meg hadn't said where in Keeper's Cottage. Was it conceivable that years ago some murdering farm-hand had buried his wife there? On balance, he reluctantly decided that it was unlikely, though not completely impossible. Monica! After a passage of twenty-six months it was an effort to recall her surname. Then it came to him. Price. Monica Price.

Chapter 2

On Wednesday morning on his way from hall to dining-room Ashley's path was bisected by Hexham bearing the newspapers to the Red Man's suite. The white-coated figure murmured good-morning, made a perfunctory gesture of standing aside to give Ashley free passage; Ashley grudgingly gave him the obligatory nod. Of all the Red Man's spies, he counted Hexham the most deadly: a creep lodged under the same roof, busy feathering his own nest, and forever fawning round Meg.

Meg poured coffee, one side of her hair lathered with cereal Pip had deposited there, vaguely conscious that her cotton blouse should, by rights, have been in the laundry basket instead of on her back. And another scorching day; the heat wave was beginning to get her down.

She sighed. "I do wish you were one of those husbands who had bacon and eggs for breakfast. I can't bear sending you off to work on a slice of toast. It's not as though you ate a proper lunch."

It was such an outworn argument that Ashley didn't exert himself to reply. Though five minutes would have brought him home for lunch, he preferred to eat at The George rather than risk a summons to the Red Man's bedside by the way of an order issued through the door into the hall he insisted should be ajar except when Hexham was engaged upon one of the obscene rituals that kept him alive.

Meg pressed hopefully: "It's so hot, wouldn't you rather come home today? It'll be cool on the terrace by noon. I'll ice some lager for you."

"No, don't bother. I'm in and out of The George in ten minutes. Honestly, I can't spare longer."

He gave her a wryly forbearing smile for her lack of wifely understanding, all the while trying to sew up into a coherent whole the disconnected shards of the dream from which he'd been shot into waking, suffused with the bounding relief that must come to a prisoner when he steps out of gaol. He'd done it, but how? Only one sequence was clear, three-dimensional: himself standing with bowed head in the hall watching the Red Man's coffin being carried out to the waiting hearse, constrained to hide from sight his suffocating jubilation because the objective that was rarely far from his mind was triumphantly achieved.

But the means he'd used to kill the Red Man? That remained buried past redemption in sleep, which meant he was thrown back into the half-baked schemes he ran through daily like a prescribed set of scales: how to contrive the Red Man's death so that it appeared an accident. Each was dog-eared with being mauled to rag-ends; all were given the kiss of death by the white-coated figure who slept, ate in the bedroom leading out of the Red Man's bathroom, a watch-dog never absent from his post.

He held out his cup for a refill. "Doesn't Hexham ever take any leave nowadays? It must be over a year since he had as much as a weekend away. I ran into him in the hall just now and it struck me he looked as pale as a piece of mouldy cheese."

Meg frowned. "I have mentioned it to him once or twice, though not lately. With Dr Pratt round the corner, and if Sister Melton comes in to give me a hand, he knows I can manage perfectly well. Last time I raised the subject, he said he didn't want to go away, that he was quite happy as long as he could go into Helton by bus one afternoon each week to change his library books and have his walk in the evening. But you're right. He should have a holiday. I'll have another go at him."

"You do, and be firm, as much for your sake as his. You don't want him cracking up."

He dropped a kiss on the side of her head free from cereal, saluted Pip, departed with the preoccupied air of a harassed executive facing a heavy day, though actually it expressed no more than maddening frustration because the life-saving inspiration he needed had struck in sleep, then floated out of reach.

Ashley, a fastidious eater, scorned The George's pre-cooked, inadequately re-heated meals, lunched on a snack at the bar. Rosie, the barmaid, who'd never see fifty again, had retained an appreciative eye for a good-looking male, a soothing manner: she served his third double with no coy hint that it would do well to be his last. As she put the roast-beef sandwich under his nose, Ashley reflected that, except she was twenty-five years too old, had to home-tint her hair, was without visible evidence of a waist, she was a paragon among women.

"Just as you like it, Mr Jones, underdone but not too raw. I hope this heat wave's not upsetting the baby? Such a lovely little fellow."

Ashley accepted the compliment with suitable modesty, added that Pip seemed to be bearing up under the hot weather.

Discreetly, Rosie made a few dabs at her mottled features. "All right if you're lucky enough to be on holiday, but it's a different story if you're on your feet all day . . . especially my poor old feet. Why, here's Mr West." She beamed. "It isn't often he honours us at lunchtime."

Come to crow, Ashley knew, as Tony West hopped with ostentatious agility on to the stool beside him.

Dapper was the adjective Tony West called to mind. Not fat, but over-plump in proportion to his five foot five inches. He claimed to be thirty-two, but who was to know! The slightly cat-like, neat-featured face, pampered with after-shave wasn't easy to slot into a definite age category. Since he made his living selling dreams of escape to the wind and the heath, he was careful to dress the part in worn but well-cut light tweeds, a tightly knotted Guards tie, old but good-quality brogues. The final note of affectation was a fisherman's fly stuck in his hat-band. Nodding a greeting Ashley repressed a shudder at the vulgarity of the carefully induced wave over his forehead.

In a hearty, ringing voice designed to impress his good humour on everyone within earshot, Tony began: "Rosie, my pigeon, what do you recommend? Tempt me not with pies, have to watch the old calories. Can you do a plate of cold meat, a bite of salad? And a pint of my usual to be going on with."

When it was drawn he raised his glass to Ashley. "Cheers."

"Cheers," Ashley replied, and left the opening move to Tony.

Tony made it without delay. "Had a session with the Old Man this morning." He paused for a comment, when it failed to emerge, continued: "Found him in splendid form. He may be lying there like a log but there's nothing wrong with his brain box. It's still popping. Amazing, don't you agree?"

Ashley did.

"He was bucked about the Sprite I off-loaded yesterday; still more by the prospect I've got of selling one of the big six-berths." He drank deeply, delicately wiped his pouting mouth before enquiring as innocently as if he didn't know the answer in advance: "How's business on your side of the fence?"

"So so. I've no complaints."

Which was a deliberate provocation for Tony to reply: "Ho, ho, but the Old Man has." Because, of course, the object of Tony's summons to Laburnum Lodge was a detailed examination of Ashley's sins of omission and commission. Tony by-passed the temptation. "By the way, I happened to run into Meg as I was leaving. She was looking an absolute peach."

Which was Tony's neatly camouflaged comeback. Meg had never looked in the least like a peach, never would, as Tony well knew. To marry the boss's daughter, live on hope of riches to come, Ashley had been forced to take to his bosom a plain wife, a girl lacking sophistication or social nous, of whom, if you were honest, the highest compliment you could pay her was that she had a clear complexion, a fine set of even white teeth and a kindly disposition.

The irony was that, given the chance, Tony would have jumped at Meg. Had, no doubt, been working up to it that day he'd begged: "Be a pal. I'm taking the Gasson girl out tonight, but it's the first time and she insists on bringing her girl friend along. Libby Soames. You know her, that gorgeous red-head with plenty of zing. Boy, am I doing you a favour!"

During the course of the evening Ashley had stage-managed a switch of partners for which Libby Soames had never forgiven him. Four months later he'd married Meg, and Tony, being Tony, had hired himself out as a spy in the hot war between Ashley and the Red Man.

Right from the word go, Ashley had accepted that in marrying Meg Gasson, the one patch of thin ice under him was that he'd be living a bare twenty miles from Helton. A nought added would have widened his safety margin, removed him from the orbit of old friends busy grinding the edges of their private grudges against him.

So far his luck had held. Naturally, the Red Man, in the short interim between engagement and marriage, had hired himself a private eye, screened him as thoroughly as if he were applying for a job with M.I.5. And wasted his money. There'd been nothing positively criminal to uncover, and Meg hadn't been in the mood to listen to a string of peccadilloes. To her, Ashley was a man who'd sown his wild oats, was ripe for reformation at her hands. She'd got a tremendous kick out of forgiving him his past.

Tony was saying: "What about little Crumley getting itself on the front pages! Did you read 'all about it' this morning?"

Ashley, as was his habit, had skimmed the morning papers at his desk while Mrs Wisley had taken pains to interrupt him a dozen times. News Editors had allotted the Reservoir Murder an average of a column, most of it couched in police jargon. He still wasn't absolutely convinced the corpse was Monica's. Clinging to the hope it was another woman's he eschewed any pressure towards panic.

Tony, without waiting for a reply, continued with his usual zest for airing his superior knowledge: "It's a challenge, a case like this, with a body over two years old. Puts the Pathology boys, the forensic lads on their mettle. Teeth!" His slightly protuberant blue eyes glinted with pride as he pronounced: "Teeth, that's the ace up their sleeve."

Ashley queried: "Teeth!"

"Sure, teeth! First job is to identify her, isn't it? Until they do that they haven't a hope of finding whoever bumped her off. Hence, teeth. They're practically indestructible." He munched the last slice of meat, looked yearningly at a roll, then self-righteously away. "Fillings, especially. Dentists keep a record of them: practically as good as fingerprints."

Noticing Ashley's taken-aback expression, he crowed: "I'd have you know that when it comes to crime you're consulting an expert." He snapped his fingers. "Par excellence. I bet you there's not a single who-dun-it that I haven't read. From Dorothy Sayers to Erle Stanley Gardner. You name it, chum, and I'll tell you who did it. Real-life murders, too. Recite you a list of the top twenty of the century, if you like."

"I'd no idea you were a crime addict!"

"Expert," Tony corrected happily. "No reason why you should. I've never pretended *my* life was an open book!" The needle of sarcasm jabbed in, he recovered his good humour, offered: "Actually, I could paint you a pretty clear picture of what the police are up to as of this minute."

"Do."

"By this evening they'll know her age, the colour of her hair, height, build, whether she ever broke any bones, had an op, though that depends to a degree upon whether there was any flesh to work on. Probably be a limited amount. Sergeant Trent told me over a pint in here last night that there was a lot of sand among the stones packed over her. Even under water that acts as a preservative." With the air of a politician reaching his punch line, he waved his hand. "Then, even though her clothes will have rotted, there'll be the tell-tale fragments of metal: hooks, buckles, zips, jewellery, say a wedding ring. They'll know how she died, whether she was strangled, shot, or cracked on the skull. Next on the agenda is the Missing Persons list. Then the real sleuthing starts."

Ashley jibed: "You astound me. I never knew you were a policeman at heart!"

For a second, resentment chilled the popping blue eyes, but it did not extend to his voice. Tony wasn't the kind to advertise ill will. "You know what I've been thinking? If she was a Helton bird, and chances are she was, it's on the cards I knew her. Two years dead. Well, I've lived in Helton for over three." He slanted his gaze directly into Ashley's. "Come to think of it, the same goes for you. As a bachelor gay you certainly played the field. Suppose you knew her, eh?"

Ashley laughed to show tolerance at the absurdity of the suggestion. "What makes you sure she's a Helton girl?"

"A hunch, boy," Tony said solemnly. "And I tell you, when it comes to murder my hunches are good. We'll know before long. Care to place a little bet?"

"I don't bet!"

"That's right, not one of your sins, is it!" Tony mashed up his paper napkin. "Must be off. Got a potential customer rolling up at two. Coming back to the grindstone?"

"Not for another five minutes. See you."

Tony grabbed his phony fisherman's hat, rammed it on at a rakish angle, quipped slyly: "Nice to be some folks! Ta-ta."

Ashley, refusing Rosie's offer of another drink, lit a cigarette and stared into a vapourising cloud of smoke trying to conjure up Monica's face. His recall, considering the lapse of time, was remarkably good. Wide cheekbones below hazel eyes that could melt from sullenness to passionate sensuality—and in reverse—in the twist of a second. Nose, too bulbous at the tip, poor complexion, but a good-shaped, fleshy mouth. Hair shoulder length, a streaky mess, sometimes pinned up, sometimes hanging down. In his mind's eye he made the mouth stretch to a smile, but the teeth she bared remained a blur. Had Monica ever visited a dentist? Prick a finger, touch a hot pan, and she'd scream in agony. Could be, if it was her corpse they'd dug up, Tony's dentist theory would fall down.

He tipped Rosie so generously, said goodbye with such an outflow of charm that her eyes hung on him until he passed out of sight. Say what you like, he was her idea of a gentleman. That smile, it fair turned your heart over. She'd ask him one day why he'd never gone into films. Of course, he hadn't done too badly for himself. Everyone said that in one way and another Mr Gasson had made a tidy pile; some that Mr Jones had married Meg to make sure of inheriting it. But she didn't believe it.

Ashley's two-minute walk to the Motor Showrooms took him past the news agent. The morning placards lettered "Reservoir Murder" were still on display. He wondered, still without undue agitation, whether Tony's crystal-ball predictions of police activity had been accurate, when they would get around to announcing the name of the victim. And if it were Monica . . . For Monica Price was assuredly dead. He should know since he put her into her grave. What he didn't know for certain was if he'd murdered her.

The news-headlined drought had burnt all life out of the lawn, reduced the herbaceous border to wilting stalks topped by parched buds unable to suck sufficient moisture from the soil to break into flower. Meg dragged a deckchair into the only patch of shade, set up Pip's play-pen. He was still drowsy after his nap, content to lie and gaze at the shifting patterns of leaves above his head. She wondered if infants of eleven months were capable of the act of thought. You read such weird theories that if you believed half of them, you'd be scared to have a baby at all.

She flipped open the writing-pad. Putting in the date her attention was deflected by a long, faded streak in her cotton skirt. She'd bought it before she'd met Ashley. By rights it ought to have been thrown out years ago. It was crazy the way she couldn't break the habit of hoarding any garment she'd worn when she'd been specially happy; as though the cloth were impregnated with a tangible essence of an hour buried in the past and she must forever be sniffing it. She'd been wearing that particular skirt when she'd walked home from Dr Pratt's surgery, so it contained an echo of his voice saying: "No doubt about it, Mrs Jones. And all as it should be. I'll want you to come for a check-up every month."

She jeered at herself: fancy turning a faded skirt into a kind of holy relic. It was the same with the silk jersey dress she'd worn the night Ashley had proposed it hung in the back of her wardrobe. But not her lace wedding gown; that she'd presented to Elsie, the cleaning woman, for her daughter to be married in. Its essence had been tainted by her father's invisible presence brooding over the church, the echo of his parting words: "Meg, for God's sake use your head! It's not too late to change your mind."

She measured the stillness of the afternoon: not a sound, even the air insulated against disturbance by the layers of heat. Resolutely she bent over the pad, then immediately lifted her head, alerted by a flicker of movement to her left, in the greenhouse that, robbed of her father's care, was fast turning into a shambles. She didn't have to guess who it was: Hexham watering down the concrete floor to cool the tomatoes. It was one of the many chores outside his nursing duties he took upon himself. She was always trying to thank him, but his reserve was so hard set that her thanks had the habit of bouncing back in her face. It wasn't that he was ever rude; rather that he was so pathologically determined to avoid attention that he'd brought to a fine art the ability to remain a shadow-figure that merged into the background. When he'd first come, she'd worried, tried to tempt him into friendliness. Now she'd given up, was content to thank heaven for him.

With Ashley's remarks at breakfast still fresh in her mind, she called: "Mr Hexham, bring a chair and come and sit in the shade with me. I want to talk to you."

The sound of her voice struck him into a rigidity that suggested the invitation posed a decision, but he brought a chair, set it up beside her without tangling the slats as most people did. Then his hands, as you would expect in someone doing his job, were dexterous and immensely strong.

She enveloped him in the friendly smile that made you forget Meg Jones was a homely-looking girl. "Now, for heaven's sake relax for half an hour. I don't know how you manage to keep continually on the go in this heat. Daddy won't need you for a while, will he?"

He answered, his eyes focused on the baby who was in the process of rolling on to his stomach: "I don't think so. In any case I can hear his bell from here."

Roger Hexham had a low-pitched, well-modulated voice in keeping with his appearance that was never other than composed. A young man of medium height, he was compactly built in proportion, with thick brown hair sleekly cut over a wide brow that jutted forward over slate-grey eyes so quiet they appeared expressionless. His features were pleasantly cast, except for his mouth, which he kept too tightly compressed. Meg's reaction when Dr Pratt had presented Hexham to her had been that he'd be downright good-looking when he smiled. That was before she learned that a smile from Hexham was a rarity. Not that he was ever surly or grudging in his manner, merely excessively grave, suggesting that no matter what he was doing the thoughts in his head claimed first priority. What on earth were they? According to Dr Pratt he was twenty-eight. So what was he doing without a girl-friend? With a lapse into schoolgirl melodrama she toyed with the idea that perhaps he had a wife somewhere from whom he was tragically separated. Say, because she was incurably insane.

He remarked: "How handsome Pip grows!"

"Thank you, Mr Hexham. What a nice compliment! Luckily he takes after his father. I do wish I had some pictures of my husband when he was a baby so that I could compare the two of them."

"You haven't?"

"No. Sad, isn't it? He lost both parents about the time he left school, and all the photographs, family treasures disappeared when the home was sold. He was too young to realise their value. Then, men aren't as sentimental as women, are they?"

Taking it as a statement rather than a question, he made no reply. Glancing at her pad, he demurred: "You mustn't let me disturb your letter-writing."

"You're a heaven-sent excuse to postpone it. I was only writing to Daddy's sister. She's a widow. Lives all alone in Hull and panics, gets on the telephone if I don't send her a bulletin once a week. That's no good because she's so deaf I can't make her hear." She twiddled her pen, went on: "There isn't anything new to tell her, is there? Dr Pratt says there isn't."

After a moment's consideration he answered: "Not really. Some days are easier for him than others. The heat tries him, but less now he's got the electric fan."

She burst out: "Mr Hexham, I realise he's a madly difficult patient, what with his moods and the rages he flies into. He can't seem to help them somehow: it's as if there's a volcano inside him and every so often it blows up. All his life he's been convinced he knows better than anyone on every subject under the sun. It must make him hard to nurse."

He said quietly: "Please don't worry, Mrs Jones. Your father is by no means the most trying patient I've nursed. The last one, for instance, was much more taxing."

"The old gentleman in Helton who died? Dr Pratt told me about him. He'd lost his mind, hadn't he?"

"He was senile."

"How sad!" she said dutifully before she broached the subject Ashley had ordered her to raise. "Mr Hexham, I'm beginning to worry about you. It's over a year, before Pip was born, since you've had any time off. It can't be good for you never getting a break. My husband was saying only at breakfast this morning you looked as if you needed a holiday."

With a sharpness that suggested not only surprise but outright offence his glance flew to her face, away again, but all he said was: "I'm fine. Stereotyped holidays aren't much in my line; I have all the free time I need."

"Nonsense," she said, digging her heels in. "Everyone needs a holiday occasionally. When you first came you used to visit your mother in Croydon. You don't even do that now! And you don't have to worry about my coping. Sister Melton will come in morning and evening, and Dr Pratt is practically next door. It's not even as though I were alone in the house at night. I have my husband. Please, Mr Hexham, I'm going to insist."

He said staring fixedly at the baby: "You mean to be kind. I appreciate it, but I assure you I'm perfectly happy with the present arrangements."

"But I'm not. If you won't go away for a week or a fort-night, I'm going to insist that you have a free weekend. We'll fix it now: the one after next. I'll phone Sister Melton as soon as I go in. You're to go away on Friday evening and forget all about us until Monday morning. That's settled."

But it wasn't. Doggedly he went on protesting until in desperation she had to threaten to summon Dr Pratt as an ally. When he grudgingly conceded defeat, she was left exhausted by the effort victory had entailed. Looking at his taut, withdrawn expression, she thought with bewilder-ment: he's as played out as I am. It was as though they had been forced into a ferocious contest of wills. And over what? A two-day break. As if for some extraordinary reason Hex-ham couldn't bear to be away from the house. Which was crazy.

The air was jarred by the ring of Frederick Gasson's bell. Hexham stood up, but paused before he hurried towards the house, said quietly: "Mrs Jones, I don't mean to be awkward about taking a short leave. But I wouldn't like anything to happen to upset you while I was away."

When he'd gone she turned the extraordinary remark over in her head. What did he mean? With Dr Pratt, Sister Mel-ton on call, Ashley and herself never stirring out of the house, her father was protected against every crisis except sudden death. Really, he was an odd person: tied up in knots inside . . . queer. No, that was a horrid word. Remind herself of his unfailing patience, forbearance with her father, his nursing skill, set them against his stony reserve.

Dr Pratt had highly recommended Roger Hexham. His references from the families of two elderly patients who had died under his care had been impeccable. So why fret because she hadn't a clue as to what went on inside his head!

Sensible, as always, she decided not to, but his patent aloneness, rigid self-containment had the effect of leaving her vaguely uneasy. She picked up her son, and as a talisman against fate, hugged him to her. How dreadful, how past bearing it would be if she lost Ashley and Pip, became like Roger Hexham, not only unloved but seemingly not wanting to be loved!

Chapter 3

On Friday morning Vanessa, tripping up the outside staircase to Stores, sighted Mr Jones parking his car, angled her
head to block his view if he chanced to look up. He did and
his slow-breaking smile made her day. A living dream, that's
what Mr Jones was.

Ashley pocketed his car keys. Long legs, narrow hips,
sweet little breasts, that yes-note in her eye. And, alas, for
him forbidden fruit. It was the apex of the Red Man's ambition that one of his spies should present him with a first-
hand account of Ashley atumble in the hay with a girl. But
he'd got that gun spiked. As long as the Red Man breathed
he'd sentenced himself to marital fidelity.

He noticed the blur of a human male shape behind the
glass partition before Mrs Wisley stumped in and, obviously
hopeful that retribution had caught up with him at last, announced: "Sergeant Curtis to see you, Mr Jones. He's from
Helton County Police. A detective!"

"Wheel him in," he replied so genially that her disappointment was visible. "I was expecting a visit from the
police."

Their arrival had become inevitable with the morning
announcement that the murdered woman had been iden-

tified as Monica Price who had erstwhile resided in Durham Road, Helton. She had been reported missing by her landlady, Mrs Josephine Warren, on the 12th June, two years ago, having a fortnight previously, without notice, vacated her room, abandoned her personal effects. It was with the object of impounding these in lieu of rent owed that Mrs Warren had resorted to the police, but Mrs Price had proved untraceable. Now the police were anxious to contact her husband, anyone who could provide them with useful information concerning the murdered woman's movements after she'd left her last-known address. Tests had established time of death as approximately two years ago—shortly after she'd disappeared from Durham Road. Cause of death: a heavy blow on the base of the skull.

A reporter had interviewed Charles Sheldock, the last owner of Dene Farm and Keeper's Cottage before they had been acquired by the Water Board under a compulsory purchase order. Now retired to a seaside bungalow in Redley Bay, Mr Sheldock had bristled indignation at being called upon to account for the two-year-old corpse, refused to hazard a guess as to how it got into Keeper's Cottage. He'd vacated the farm three years ago. Thereafter it became the property of the Water Board, so who had murdered whom in Keeper's Cottage was plainly no business of his, was it! Keeper's Cottage? Half-derelict for more years than he could remember. No gas, electricity, or piped water, only a muck road that bogged anything on wheels in winter. Well, in this so-called affluent society, no self-respecting farm labourer was going to live under such primitive conditions, was he? Or if he was, his wife wouldn't let him. So he'd abandoned it to nature, and when last he'd seen it, hoodlums had been giving nature a helping hand.

The editor had sniffed round the suggestion of hoodlums, come up with nothing news-worthy. When questioned, the

P.R.O. of the Water Board had been guarded in his replies. Certainly the body had been found on their property. Yes, it was logical to assume it had been buried shortly before the valley was flooded. They were, naturally, in contact with the police, supplying them with what data they required. At this stage, the Water Board preferred to make no further comment.

Monica, Ashley thought savagely, damn her to hell, rising up to threaten him from beyond the grave he'd piled over her. How he'd schemed to silence her menacing tongue was sharply etched in his memory, spot-lighted even at a distance by the glow of exultation he'd felt as he'd checked over and over the plan until it was perfect. And it had worked like a dream until that missing cog had faced him with a gigantic question mark. Had he killed her, or had someone forestalled him?

Until Meg had come running into the house on Tuesday the blank space in the middle of the first act of murder hadn't bothered him unduly. Either by his hand or another's Monica had been robbed of the power of speech. But since the police had pinned Monica's name on the bones they'd unearthed, he had put intense pressure on his memory to supply a second-by-second visual recall of that Sunday afternoon in May.

In order to be inside the ruined cottage before Monica, he'd arrived early. But when he'd navigated the wickedly rutted cart track, driven through the screen of brambles to park on the oblong of hard-core that was probably the foundations of an old shed that had blown away in a gale years ago, Monica's empty car had already been standing there, its engine cold. No more than mildly annoyed at this disruption of his time-table, he'd parted the curtain of trailing creepers and brambles to prospect. After that nothing but a vacuum of ten to twelve minutes by his watch on which there wasn't a scribble of recollection until he'd found himself bent over her dead, disgustingly dishevelled body half in, half out of the great collapsing cavern of the fire-place inside the cottage.

When he'd recovered from the first bludgeoning shock, he'd moved like an automaton into the second act, designed to get Monica into a keeping-place where she'd lie unde-tected until the waters silently and slowly rose to hold her from sight for ever, the king-pin of his plan being that no one should suspect she was dead.

But if he hadn't killed her with the bloodstained rock that had been balanced in his hand, someone had known for twenty-six months that Monica Price had been mur-dered.

It was with this great ugly conundrum occupying the fore-front of his mind that he directed a winning smile at his interrogator, proceeded to sum him up. Totally unimpres-sive. Off-the-peg navy suit, a fraction skimpy over his shoulders. Thirty-ish. Conventional policeman's dead-pan face. Small eyes, mouth revealing a tooth that needed re-capping, but, ah, a pugnacious jaw-line.

Ashley wondered if there was an army of Sergeant Curtis's, methodically questioning every male who'd as much as passed the time of day with Monica, or if he'd been singled out for preferential treatment. What was be-yond doubt was that Sergeant Curtis would have conscien-tiously done his homework on Ashley Jones, have his background filed away in his head. Well, forearmed, he counted himself a match for any policeman in or out of uniform.

He held out his cigarette case, and when the offer was refused, asked helpfully: "Well, Sergeant, what can I do for you?"

Curtis flapped open his notebook, said with prim police

formality: "My visit concerns Monica Price, the woman whose body we found on Tuesday afternoon. I understand you were acquainted with her?"

"Yes, I knew Monica. If you hadn't looked in, I was considering whether I hadn't a duty to contact you." He shook his head in pained revulsion. "Ghastly business. I suppose you're quite sure?"

"Quite, sir. How well did you know her?"

"She was a friend." He paused, emphasised: "Please note, Sergeant, that I'm using the word in its literal meaning. A friend, no more. Monica had a considerable number of whom I happened to be one." He stared into mid-air, appearing to calculate. "I suppose I knew her for about a year . . . no, a little longer than that. I first ran into her at the Pelican. I expect you know it, the pub in the market place. I forget who introduced us. Probably Tony West, though I can't swear to it. But he certainly knew her before I did. From then on we met here and there. In the Pelican, at parties in Tony's flat, my place."

Curtis consulted a note. "Her landlady states that she vacated her room during the weekend of May twenty-eighth to thirtieth. Can you recall when you last saw Mrs Price?"

Ashley expostulated good-humouredly: "My dear Sergeant, you must be joking! Over two years ago. Perhaps I should explain that around that time I was looking forward to becoming engaged." He smiled meaningfully at Sergeant Curtis. When Curtis did not smile back, he went on soberly: "I'm sorry, but I couldn't even hazard a guess at the date. All I do remember is that the last time I did see her she was talking vaguely about trying to land a job in London as a hotel receptionist, which is why I wasn't surprised to hear she'd left Helton. I assumed she'd got it, buzzed off."

"Leaving all her belongings, sir? Even her toothbrush!"

"Look, Sergeant, I'm not one to malign the dead. I certainly wouldn't wish to speak one uncharitable word about Monica, but since you'll discover it for yourself, I'm giving nothing away if I tell you Monica was never out of debt. A few clothes, personal bits and bobs in exchange for arrears of rent! Well, it figures, don't you think?"

"Did she borrow money from you, sir?"

"A few pounds. . . . She cadged small amounts off most of the gang at the Pelican. Again, I assumed she'd run out of credit, made off to fresh fields."

"Did she ever mention her husband, say whether he was dead, or there had been a divorce?"

"Never, Sergeant."

"Give you any idea whether Price was her married or single name?"

"No." Ashley smiled with conscious knowingness. "But presumably, from records that you'll consult, you'll be able to find that out for yourselves!"

Curtis, rather ostentatiously, made no answer. Visibly bracing himself, he delivered his main plea: "Mr Jones, can you recall any fact concerning Mrs Price that would suggest she was on ill terms with anyone? Did you ever hear of a quarrel between her and a man with whom she'd been intimate?"

Ashley mashed out his cigarette, shook his head in a slow motion of regret. "I only wish I could help. But Monica and I had no reason to keep tags on one another. She wasn't a girl given to confidences. I got the idea that she jibbed rather at talking about the past, because for some reason she kept to herself she found it painful. When we'd be having a drink, she'd spend most of the time grousing about her current job; she had half a dozen different ones while I knew her. She never considered any of them were worthy of her. In some ways, she was still a bit of a mixed-up kid."

"I see," said Curtis dourly.

"Sorry, Sergeant, I'm not being much help, am I! I hope you strike luckier with her other friends. I could give you a list, but maybe you've got one already?"

"Her landlady and the woman who rented the room above Mrs Price's have been helpful. It was Mrs Warren who put us in touch with Mr West."

"And Mr West suggested you should see me?"

"That's right, sir."

"Very sensible. But, frankly, Sergeant, apart from what I've already told you, I'm a dead loss."

Curtis put away his notebook. "If anything should occur to you, sir, for instance the approximate date of the last occasion on which you spoke to the deceased, perhaps you'd be good enough to get in touch with us. Helton 219. Detective Superintendent Ross is handling the case. If he isn't available, you should ask for me or Detective Sergeant Hallam."

"I'll make a note." Ashley did so, aware of the professionally blank eyes that even with their interview ended were doggedly keeping him under surveillance, as though reluctant to let him off the hook.

"I hope you catch the brute who killed her. Monica had her faults—who hasn't—but she didn't deserve that. What a filthy end!"

"Yes, sir. Good day, Mr Jones."

When he was alone, under the shield of the desk that screened his hands from Mrs Wisley's zealous spying, he wiped the palms. Funny, he hadn't been conscious of being under pressure, yet he'd sweated. Put it down to the nerve-strain of giving a superb performance. Now for Tony.

He found him at his desk in his pre-fabricated cedar-wood office sited at the base of the caravan park, his normal ebullience noticeably dimmed, sagging like a balloon with a slow leak.

"Monica! Poor old Monica!" He beat his forehead with a clenched fist. "Who the hell could have wanted to kill Monica?"

Ashley sat down in the client's chair. "I thought you were the expert!"

Tony glared resentfully. "It's hardly a subject for joking!"

"Who's joking. Certainly not that detective you sent to grill me. How many other names did you give him?"

Tony's gaze wandered evasively round the small room, taking pains not to make contact with Ashley's. "The rest of the Pelican gang. I hadn't any choice. Anyway, what's the harm? With Ross on the case, they'd have got them from someone else. He's the one who caught Lexton, the man who knifed the police cadet last year, and Peter Coby who raped and strangled little Jane Bates."

Hoisted on his hobby-horse, he retrieved some of his old spirit, said self-importantly: "Ross always gets his man. That's what shot him ahead. He's as proud as a peacock because he's solved every murder case he's handled . . . doesn't want to spoil his record."

Even so, it was with visible relief that Tony smiled a welcome at Vanessa who was poised with artless grace on the threshold. "What is it, love?"

"A Mr and Mrs Watson to see you. They say they telephoned to make an appointment."

"Indeed they did. Bring them along." He passed a hand over his hair to slick it smooth, rose briskly to his feet, started busily to shuffle papers round his desk. "Sorry, old man, I'll have to ask you to excuse me."

To Ashley, Tony's obvious gratitude for the reprieve afforded by the arrival of Mr and Mrs Watson was a definite pointer that he'd been at pains to lay before Sergeant Curtis as many damning facets of Ashley Jones's relationship with Monica as he could call into his tiny mind. Ashley smiled to himself. But not one word about the new relationship that had erupted during the last three weeks of Monica's life . . . for the simple reason that Tony couldn't know of its existence. No one did. Her own interest would have muzzled Monica's tongue, and he'd taken elaborate pains to keep it hidden from every spying eye. The crumbled walls of Keeper's Cottage couldn't talk to Tony or the police. So why was he worrying? He decided he wasn't. He was simply damning to hell an Act of God that no man could have been expected to foresee.

Driving back to Laburnum Lodge on Friday evening, Ashley schooled himself to face a Red Man convulsed by demoniacal rage. Monica Price's name had figured on the list of the six girls the Red Man had brandished triumphantly under Meg's nose as proof that Ashley Jones wasn't a fit husband for any self-respecting woman. He'd have read his newspapers. Between 1 and 1.30, when she was alone in the office, Mrs Wisley would have reported by telephone to the Red Man that his son-in-law had been questioned by a plain-clothes policeman. All told, a Red Letter day for the Red Man. Ashley had spent a considerable portion of the afternoon marshalling his defence.

It transpired he'd wasted his time. The Red Man, most uncharacteristically, was off the boil. A log who emitted a series of grunts, made no comment on the daily reports, dismissed Ashley with a contemptuous nod.

And Meg, though the news of his police interrogation must have filtered through to her made no reference to it during dinner, supplying him instead with tid-bits of gossip. Elsie's daughter was pregnant, the postman's son had been rushed to hospital to have his appendix removed, the Harrisons up the road were cursing as they packed to fly off to Spain that they hadn't spent their holiday money on building a swimming pool. It couldn't be hotter, not even in Majorca.

As she brought in the ice-cream, she said: "I forgot to tell you my piece of good news. I've made Hexham promise to take a break next weekend. He's terribly obstinate, won't consider going away for longer."

"Good for you!" He smiled approval at her, while resentment churned in him at the vicious kick from fate that had embroiled him in two crises simultaneously: Monica's murder, which should have been buried beyond recall in the past, and his frantic need to rid himself of the Red Man's stranglehold.

Fine that Hexham's absence from the house was ensured, but infuriating that he remained devoid of inspiration how to exploit it. However ferociously he pursued it, the sequence of the dream in which he'd contrived the Red Man's accidental demise refused to recur, spell out the means he'd used.

"How long will he be away? Three nights?"

"No, only two, Friday and Saturday, and I'm not even sure now about Friday. He's already started hinting that he doesn't want to leave till Saturday, and he insists on being back Sunday night."

As Meg performed the rite of stirring sugar into Ashley's cup before she set it before him, she counselled herself to restraint. At all costs, she must not sound worried. But some comment had to be made. A girl Ashley had been on friendly terms with before their marriage had been murdered: it was inhuman not to mention it. The problem was that she badly needed Ashley to provide her with a guideline by his words, tone of voice. Disbelief, horror, pity, which was he feeling? It would happen to be one of those evenings when, unless she chattered like mad, communication between them went to sleep.

She teased: "Lovey, you're miles away. Tell me where you've gone to."

He slanted his head towards her, allowed time for his most mesmerising smile to cast its spell, before he said softly: "Pink, that particular shade of coral, rose, whatever it is, is your colour. You look beautiful tonight."

"Liar!" She pulled a cushion to his feet, sat on it. "I'm plain Jane and you know it. Draping me in mink and diamonds wouldn't make me beautiful. Tell me what you were really thinking."

"Wishing we could take off in the car for Spain, just you and me."

She sighed. "Me, too. It would be heaven. But we can't take Pip until he's older, and I couldn't bear to leave him. Anyway . . ."

Anyway the Red Man couldn't be abandoned, he silently finished for her. He left a pause before he said casually: "By the way, I'll have to leave you for ten minutes to slip out to The George. I've run out of cigarettes."

Though she kept a supply for visitors in the grocery cupboard, she didn't offer him a packet because it wasn't cigarettes he wanted. Not to worry, she scolded herself. It wasn't a crime for a man to prefer a drink in a pub with his cronies once in a while to the company of his wife. She'd learnt, so painfully that the knowledge seemed old now, that there was no equality in loving. One loved; one was loved. Once you'd tumbled to that you stopped feeling sorry for yourself.

But when Ashley got to his feet, the question she'd been holding back since he arrived home jumped out of her mouth. "Ashley, that woman who was murdered, the newspapers say she was Monica Price."

The blue eyes between their dark lashes became grave

to the point of sadness. "I know. I still can't believe it."

"They seem absolutely sure."

"So the detective said when he called to see me this morning. But I still find it hard to accept."

"What did he want, the detective who came to see you?"

"Background stuff. They're questioning everyone who knew her, trying to build up a picture of what she did, where she went after she left her room." He gave her a look of amazement. "You're not worrying, you can't be? You are! Because that broken-down private-eye your father hired put Monica down as one of a dozen girls I'd had a drink with!"

"No," she said hotly. "I'm not worried. I know that stupid man wilfully exaggerated, put the worst possible complexion on . . . well . . . everything."

He said with dignity: "You have my word, there wasn't anything but casual friendship between us. Either you believe me or Eric Dodge."

"I believe you. You know that." Miserably she tried to explain. "I think it's because it was such a particularly beastly murder that I can't get it out of my head. I keep thinking: supposing she wasn't dead when she was buried, only stunned." She clapped her hands to her cheeks in horror.

"That," he said firmly, "is merely being morbid. Monica has been dead for over two years. Naturally everyone who knew her is upset, bending over backwards to give the police all the help they can in catching whoever murdered her. Hysterics are a bit silly, don't you think?"

"I'll be sensible," she said earnestly, "I really will."

Chapter 4

Five minutes after Ashley had driven away, Hexham, his white coat changed for a tan linen jacket, black shoes for a heavy-service brown pair, stood in the hall listening: absorbed in a ritual he performed each evening, to detect in which part of the house or garden he might find Meg to announce his departure on his hour's walk. Kitchen!

Water gushing from the taps into sink muffled his approach, so there was a moment when from the threshold he was free to gaze at her back, the dark hair curving raggedly into her milk-white neck, before he stepped forward, offered: "Mrs Jones, won't you please let me give you a hand."

She whirled round. "Mr Hexham! Goodness, you made me jump. You move so quietly I never hear you coming. No, of course, you can't help. I'm half-way through. You go for your walk."

"I'd like to. You must be tired."

"I am not," she said firmly. "If I wanted to I could leave them for Elsie in the morning, but I don't mind doing dishes. Making beds, dusting, those are the chores I hate." Guilty in case she'd snubbed him, she tried to make amends by asking pleasantly: "Mr Hexham, where do you go for your evening walk? Always the same way, or do you vary it?"

"I usually keep to the same route. Down Piper's Lane, across the meadows at the top, up to the Beacon. Sometimes I sit down there for a few minutes; there's a fine view of the reservoir. There and back it takes me exactly an hour."

As with most reserved people, his glance was inclined to evasiveness, and it was only when he thought she wasn't looking at him that he focused upon her that strange, intent stare that left her vaguely embarrassed. But tonight he sought her eyes with open expectation, waiting for her to pick up the word reservoir. Well, everyone in Crumley, Helton, the dozen villages scattered around, would be likely to react to it. Murder, the ultimate in sensation, universally irresistible. Except for her. Meg had no inclination to discuss Monica Price's murder with Hexham.

She said brightly: "I've been that way too. I'll go again as soon as Pip's legs have grown; it's too rough for his pushchair. Bye, and don't hurry back. As soon as I'm through here I'm going to sit with Daddy."

As always, her father had counted her steps on the woodblock floor of the hall, had his face angled on the pillow to catch the first possible sight of her face as she appeared round the half-open door. With expertise she'd learnt over three years, she analysed the quality of his smile, pronounced: "You're tired. I don't wonder in this heat, but it can't last much longer."

He growled: "I'm tired with worrying. I lie here fretting my heart out about you. Now this business!" He flicked a stubby finger to indicate the newspapers spread across the bed. "This tramp Ashley carried on with murdered! Did he tell you that the police were in his office questioning him this morning?"

"Of course he did. They're seeing everyone who knew her. It doesn't mean that you have to worry yourself sick."

"Worry!" His face swelled and darkened with the secretions of rage he tried in vain to subdue. "You tell me how I can help worrying! Where he's concerned you haven't as much sense as a six-year-old kid . . ."

"Daddy, stop it. You should know by now that I won't listen when you shout a lot of wicked lies about Ashley. He's my husband. I love him. You're so obstinately prejudiced that you can't see him as he is."

"Oh, I can see him all right. And it's because I can that I'm warning you, Meg, I've stood all I'm going to from him. If he's mixed up in this murder, I'll not lift a finger to help him."

Anger she'd vowed never to allow to break over her father, leapt out of control. She shouted: "Unless you stop, I'm going. I don't have to stay here and listen to you accusing my husband of being mixed up in a murder. Ashley hardly knew her. That amateur detective you hired lied his head off."

"All I'm doing is giving you due warning that if he as much as had a hand in this woman's death, even knew she'd been murdered, from now on, as far as I'm concerned, it's between him and the police."

She said distantly: "For the last time Ashley had nothing to do with it. He didn't even know she was dead. Now do you want me to read to you, or would you like the television on?"

He turned his head away, grunted: "Please yourself."

She moved the switch of the television. Before the sound came on, he twisted his face back towards her, the anger gone, his expression one of unyielding despair. "Meg, if you don't come to your senses pretty soon, he'll be the end of both of us. Don't you know, even yet, what he's after!"

Richard Price was only thirty-eight, but since his mid-twenties when his hair had turned prematurely silver he'd looked ten years older than his age. Tall and noticeably lean with a slight stoop, the effect was heightened by the type of facial structure that tends to fall into lines. His was so rutted with creases across the brow and running from nostrils to mouth that he appeared gaunt and haggard until he smiled and then, Sylvie declared, he looked like a hungry poet who'd found the right word, was all set to eat.

He stood at the window of the eighth-floor modern flat in Brighton listening to Sylvie's voice coming from across the hall where she was chiding Jinny for being disinclined for sleep.

When she comes back, he resolved, and they were alone, one of them must speak Monica's name. He turned inwards, encompassing the room with a glance of sombre passion. By any standards it was blessed with light, grace and pools of sheer beauty. But he'd have prized it as highly if it had been dark and squalid, furnished from cheap-Jack stores, because it was theirs, a sanctum for which they'd hungered in the wilderness.

He heard Sylvie close Jinny's door, said aloud to strengthen his will: "Now . . ."

But when she was framed in the doorway, her blue eyes darkened with alarm that must have settled there with the morning paper that arrived after he left for the office, her gilt, thistledown hair outlining a face that reminded him of an angel's in a Fra Angelico painting, his tongue stayed dumb. It would be easier to die than to hurt her.

She stepped towards him slowly, giving him time to witness the blenching of her rose-toned skin, the tightening of her lovely mouth. Because her courage was greater than his, he knew she was going to speak first. It was only the fury behind her denunciation that caught him by surprise.

"She couldn't even die decently! She had to get herself murdered, spread over the front page of every rubbishy newspaper. Ricky, I don't think I can bear it."

"Hush!" He held out his arms. "There's nothing for you to bear. She's dead, that's all there is to it."

With her head pressed into his shoulder, the voice he hated rang mockingly in his head. Monica had called out: "Why hello! What a lovely surprise! Pardon me if I remark that the world is a *very* small place."

She'd been sitting at the wheel of her car parked next to his, a sly smile on her face because she knew it wasn't surprise that locked his tongue but a shocking fear that he despised in himself, as he strove to decide whether it was a genuine encounter or whether she'd seen him park behind his office in the morning, planted herself there to wait for his return in the evening? He'd had to force his head into a jerky nod of greeting.

"Living by the sea now, are you! I guess Sylvie likes that. It's terrible, but I've forgotten whether the infant was a boy or a girl. Which was it?"

"A girl."

"How nice for you both. I don't suppose you feel inclined to buy me a drink for old times' sake? No, I thought not. Well, you never know, we may meet up again some time."

He'd prayed not. But there hadn't been a hope, and in his heart he'd always known it. Once she'd found out the town to which he'd fled, a flick through a telephone directory would give her his address if she wanted to misuse it, and of course she had. In retrospect that turned his decision not to change his name into a bad misjudgement. But who wanted to take on a man who'd worked for his previous employer under a different name?

Sylvie drew back, calmer now, braced for the worst. "It

says that the police want you to get in touch with them. Ricky, are you going to?"

He smiled comfort at her. "Darling, it would be pointless, wouldn't it? I couldn't tell them anything; I haven't seen her for six years."

She said wonderingly, searching his face: "You mean we don't have to get involved? We haven't a thing to worry about?"

"Not a thing."

Though Tony lived in Helton, he spent odd evenings drinking at The George, and Ashley's object in going down there was to press on with their short-circuited conversation of the morning. While discounting a percentage of Tony's bragging, it did appear that he was, to a degree, surprisingly well-informed on police procedure—witness his familiarity with Ross's record. Ashley badly wanted to know, in fact needed to know, what was cooking. For instance, who else in Crumley besides himself and Tony had been favoured with a visit from Sergeant Curtis? Failing Tony, there was always the chance that Sergeant Trent might be pontificating over a pint.

In fact, neither was visible when he pushed his way into the crowded Saloon. A couple of feet from the bar he collided with a shoulder, found himself looking down into a dark-skinned, grimly set visage. Tom Norris, the Red Man's head mechanic and number four spy, was so tight with words he'd never been known to throw one away. "Evening" was the sole response Ashley received to his apology and greeting.

Thomas Nathaniel Norris, rapidly approaching fifty, widower, with a son serving in the Army of the Rhine, lived alone. Until two years ago, with the Red Man dithering between him and Tony, he must have been cherishing the hope that he stood a good chance of becoming Manager of Gasson's. Then Meg, out of a hat, had produced the perfect candidate.

Dolled up in his best, he arrived at Laburnum Lodge at noon fifty-two Sundays in the year to drink a glass of beer with the Red Man, take his leave with a cigar sticking out of his pocket in token payment for his weekly report on Ashley Jones's malpractices.

Sam Goodsell's day was Wednesday, a cribbage session from 8 to 10 P.M. during which he drank as much whisky as the Red Man was disposed to offer him, ate his way through a mountain of ham sandwiches and mumbled his grievances against Ashley Jones.

It had amused Ashley to put up a smokescreen of pretence that he and Norris formed two halves of an ideal working partnership. Never a word of criticism, never a trespassing toe, tactics that reduced Norris, a near-genius with car engines but as easy to wrong-foot as a child, to a glowering mute.

When Ashley, by right of whim, took the empty chair at a table for two at which Norris had seated himself, his mouth tightened, but he said nothing.

Ashley sipped half his drink before he enquired: "I wanted a word with West. Have you seen him in here?"

"No." Norris emptied his glass in two hefty swallows, ran the back of his hand over his mouth, rose to his feet.

Ashley smiled genially. "Don't go, Tom. Have another on me?"

"No thanks, Mr Jones."

Ashley grinned openly as, all his hackles bristling, Norris disappeared into the street, no doubt brooding that to sup with the devil you needed a long spoon.

He was at the bar ordering his second drink when a trio entered: Libby and Ian Thomas, and Prince.

Ashley snapped his fingers and with a lunge the Alsatian dragged his leash out of Ian's grasp, loped forward, his plumed tail thrashing the air, to lay his muzzle against Ashley's knee. Fondling it, the taste of deprivation was as bitter as the day it was born, in the third month of Meg's pregnancy.

Dreams come in assorted sizes. Ashley couldn't remember when he'd first dreamed of owning an Alsatian. Preoccupied in settling his marriage into shape, confounding the Red Man's predictions, he'd bided his time. The first anniversary behind him, he'd decided to award himself a bonus. When he'd casually mentioned it to Meg the possibility of opposition hadn't crossed his mind.

"I'm going to buy an Alsatian. There's a breeder at Kempton who's got a champion litter. I went over this morning, picked out the best male puppy. Silver Prince. Magnificent dog. He'll be ready to collect at the weekend."

Meg's expression became one of acute dismay. "You can't," she blurted. "I'm sorry, darling, but an Alsatian is out. You can't have one."

"Why not?"

"Daddy can't stand dogs. He wouldn't have one in the house. I'm not keen either, not on an Alsatian. Ugh, they're like wolves . . . and all those stories you read about them turning savage."

"This one won't. He's got a perfect temperament. As for your father—it's not his dog. It'll be my exclusive property. He doesn't even have to see it."

"Ashley! With his door open . . . the casement window! You couldn't keep it out of his room." She'd shaken her head unhappily. "Darling, I'm sorry, but it's not to be thought of."

He'd fought her for a week—his first, mortifying experience of the stubbornness built into her. He pulled out every stop in his repertoire, reduced her to weeping misery, but she'd still said no.

A few weeks later Silver Prince had been bought by Ian Thomas, gentleman farmer, recently married to Libby Soames, who had been his date on the evening he'd first met Meg Gasson.

Normally Libby wore her hair loose in a flaming red cloud, but tonight, because of the heat, she'd pinned it up. It was a style that showed off her marble white throat, finely moulded jaw-line. She had wide hazel eyes that in some lights turned green, slender legs and thighs that provided a nice contrast to her thirty-seven-inch bust. Since she was Meg's best friend, the three of them greeted each other with exclamations of surprised delight. It was only when they were safe from the sight and hearing of eavesdroppers that a hard glint in Libby's eyes, a biting rasp to her tongue reminded Ashley that she'd neither forgiven nor forgotten. Too bad! He counted it his loss that she'd been born Elizabeth Soames, third daughter of a bank manager in superb physical shape, unlikely to bequeath his offspring more than a pittance, instead of Meg Gasson.

While Ian ordered drinks, Libby jibed sweetly: "Prince is so touchingly devoted to you, much more so than he is to Ian, I wonder you don't buy one of his little brothers. I hear there's a new litter." She pressed a finger to her mouth in false contrition. "Oh, I forgot Meg's terrified of Alsatians, isn't she! When she comes visiting I have to tie Prince up in case he gobbles Pip for lunch."

Ian Thomas, a burly young man, with a round sunburnt face, good-humoured eyes, raised his glass: "Cheers! Libby been talking to you about tomorrow week?"

"I've scarcely had time yet, darling!"

"We're throwing a party. It's an age since we've given a big one. We've got two excuses. Harebell, bless her little

58

Jersey socks, won the top award in her class at the Counties Show, and yours truly is coming up to his thirty-fifth birthday. We're putting on a barbecue, so keep your fingers crossed the weather doesn't break. Strong drink due to start flowing at 6 P.M. That's right, isn't it, my true love?"

"Right. I meant to phone Meg today, but I've never had a moment to get around to it. You invite her for me."

Tomorrow week. Saturday. The weekend that the house was due to be swept free of Hexham's guardianship. With him absent it was unlikely that Meg would trust any babysitter living with the double charge of her father and Pip. Wait . . . could he coax her into entrusting him with the job, go to the party, leave him behind? Was a chance, *the* chance, being offered to him on a plate? But until he knew how it was to be done, how could he decide? A blaze of white-hot anger shot through him at his failure to contrive a fatal accident that would boot the Red Man off the face of the earth.

"Sounds fine," he said, playing for time. "But I'll have to check with Meg. There's a slight complication because Hexham is away that weekend, and you know how conscientious she is about her father."

"And how!" Libby drawled. "But you must use your maximum powers of persuasion, mustn't you. Then you're quite irresistible."

"Do your best, old man," Ian urged. "It wouldn't be a party without you and Meg." He drank. "By the way, what do you think about this tart being found murdered at the bottom of our reservoir? Crumley meets up with the Crime Wave, eh?"

"Tart!" Ashley queried. "Was she one?"

"My dear boy, didn't you know statistics prove that ninety per cent of women who get themselves murdered are either tarts or faithless wives!" He grinned at his own.

"The other ten is accounted for by dear old ladies who will keep bundles of banknotes sewn up in their mattresses."

Libby murmured: "Maybe Ashley wouldn't agree with you. He actually knew her. That's right, isn't it. I saw you with her at Tony's several times."

Ian goggled. "Is that a fact, that you and Tony knew her?"

"She was in and out of the Pelican where Tony and I forgathered when I lived in Helton. He invited her to drinking sessions at his flat." He turned to Libby. "You knew her too."

"Only very vaguely. We were never formally introduced."

"Poor bitch," Ian said with feeling. "Conked on the head, shoved into a grave." He beckoned Rosie. "Three more of the same as soon as you've got a minute."

Ashley put his empty glass down. "Count me out, Ian. I must be getting back home."

"Oh, must you!" Libby exclaimed with sham distress. "It's so early, only half-past nine. Or does the Ogre bolt and bar the door at ten sharp? He used to put on a terrific Mr Barrett act when Meg was at school. Indoors by nine, my girl, or a week on bread and water. Hasn't age mellowed him?"

Ian grinned amiably. "Forgive my idiot wife. She works hard at sounding witty. It's a bad habit of hers I'm trying to cure. All the best to Meg, and tell her we're counting on you for the party."

Despite Libby's smiling ridicule, he paused to run his hand over Prince's muzzle. Not Prince, Ian would never part with him, but his double, stretched at his feet on a sunlit patio, or bounding at his side as they raced neck and neck for the surf.

Hexham was back at his post, Meg in the sitting-room watching television. She snapped it off, ran towards him. In the second before she buried her head in his shoulder he noticed she'd been crying. Absently he wondered why, but did not enquire. The likeliest explanation was that the Red Man had been giving her hell.

Not wishing to commit himself either way until he had worked out whether acceptance or refusal would work to his advantage, he didn't mention the party invitation.

Undressing, he determined to sweep his mind clear of all the bedevilling implications behind the unearthing of Monica's bones, back-tracking, checking up on himself. He'd made no mistakes, left no clue for Ross and his army of policemen to pick up. So forget it. Instead, as he lay waiting for sleep, he would concentrate all his wits on devising a fatal accident that would put the Red Man's wealth within his grasp, will the whole of the dream to re-surface.

He strove until he reached the threshold of sleep, then, without a flicker of warning, a new area of thinking jumped him awake. If he hadn't murdered Monica, then the chances were that whoever had was someone he knew.

Chapter 5

Theresa Dunston's sustaining pride was that she was a lady born. Circumstances might have forced her into trade, but she had never conducted herself in a manner to dishonour the memory of her dear father, who had been an Anglican vicar.

She'd battled hard with her conscience before, on Saturday morning, she donned her navy linen suit, matching hat, best suede gloves. You stuck to your principles, obeyed the precepts in which you'd been tutored by your parents. When something unpleasant occurred you did not, if you were a Christian, draw in your skirts, look the other way. When the dead, debarred from pleading on their own behalf, were maligned, you spoke up for them.

At Helton Police Station, after she had asked to see Det. Superintendent Ross, she had to endure a stone-walling operation to her simple request that was time-wasting but ineffective. Three separate young men urged, even bullied her, to communicate her business to them. It was three-quarters of an hour before she enjoyed the triumph of being ushered into Superintendent Ross's office.

At sixty-two Theresa Dunston had a poker-straight back, no more weight on her than she'd had thirty years ago, slightly horselike features and a pair of fiercely intimidating blue eyes which she focused on the man who made a perfunctory gesture of rising from behind a desk before immediately subsiding back into his chair.

Middle-aged, substantially built except for a thin, sharp-featured face, and, judging from the yellowy tinge of his skin, a dyspeptic. The room itself was airless, not as dust-free as it might have been. The overflowing ash tray offended her nostrils and there appeared to be a dirty cup and saucer under the desk by her feet.

Invited to seat herself, she nevertheless began: "It is kind . . ."

With a peremptory gesture he interrupted her. "Perhaps you would give me your full name, address."

"Theresa Mary Dunston. My present address is the Claremont Private Hotel, the Ridge, Helton. Until just over two years ago I was the proprietor of the Gift Shop in the High Street. I'm sure you know it."

Without revealing whether he did or didn't, Ross asked on a brisk note intended as a hint that he'd appreciate brevity: "And what information have you to give me about Monica Price, Miss Dunston, that you were unwilling to impart to any of my officers?"

She raised her head slightly, pronounced with dignity: "Superintendent, I have never before entered a police station. I have brought myself to do so today because I am of the firm opinion it is my duty. On a confidential matter, I naturally prefer to deal with a departmental head rather than young boys. Slander is rife in the town, even in my hotel. It has been said in my hearing that Monica Price was no better than a streetwalker. That was not so. I employed her. Would I be likely to confront my customers with a prostitute?"

For the first time since she'd entered his office, an enigmatic half-smile relieved the taut gravity of Ross's expression. He said less tersely: "I would judge not. Please tell me what you do know about Monica Price, Miss Dunston. Suppose that you'd been asked to give her a reference, what would you have said?"

"She was an excellent saleswoman, with pleasant manners, a most satisfactory employee and a young woman who most sincerely desired to better herself."

"When you say she wanted to better herself, what precisely do you mean?"

"That it was her ambition to earn a decent salary, be done with drifting from one job to another. Unfortunately, she'd no specific training, so only a limited number of positions were open to her. She resented this, because it meant she was reduced to living in a shabby room, with no cooking facilities, sharing a bathroom with other tenants who were not always as particular in their habits as they might have been. Her aim was a job that would allow her to live decently, with security."

"An aim common to most of us, Miss Dunston. When was she in your employ and for how long?"

"Three years last April I engaged her as a temporary assistant for the summer season. In the autumn, although I would have liked to have kept her on, I was not in a position to do so, as I already had Mrs Barnes who had been with me for ten years. Mrs Price had been warned, of course, that this would be the case. But she was obviously upset, and on the day she left she asked if she could see me in my flat above the shop to discuss a personal matter. Perhaps I should explain, Superintendent, that it had been widely known that I intended in the not too distant future, to sell the shop, retire. What Monica wished to talk over was the possibility of her buying my business. I must admit that I was surprised to learn that she had the financial resources to consider such a transaction.

"When I intimated as much she said that it might be possible for her to raise a little capital, and asked what sum I had in mind. As I had already had the premises, good-will, stock valued, I told her £5,500. I'm afraid the sum involved came as a blow. She couldn't have realised until then that I owned the freehold of the premises. It was quite obvious to me that she was bitterly disappointed, but as I had privately decided not to put the shop on the market until spring, I said something to the effect that she could think it over. I certainly did not expect anything further to come of it.

"But the following May she telephoned, asked if she could come to see me to discuss the matter again. When she did so, I learned that her financial situation had changed for the better and now she had every hope of being able to raise £2,000. What she wanted to know was, if she put down this sum, would I be willing to wait twelve months for the remainder of the purchase price. Frankly, I didn't care for the idea, but she was so persistent—and I knew what acquiring the business would mean to her—that I promised to consult my bank manager, and meanwhile gave her what amounted to a month's option. We left it that during that period she would contact me again, confirm that she had actually obtained the cash needed for the deposit, and advised by the bank, I would see if something couldn't be worked out.

"She did not do so. When the month had run out, I telephoned, only to learn that she had moved away ten days previously without leaving a forwarding address. I concluded that she had been disappointed in her hope of raising the £2,000, and that she preferred not to lose face by coming and admitting it to me. A few weeks after that I sold the business to the present owner, Miss Beasby."

He asked in a voice that suggested he no longer regarded her as a tiresome intruder: "Did she give you any idea from whom she was going to obtain the money?"

"No, but she seemed quite confident of getting it. It was an expectation that made a new woman of her, as if she'd been granted a fresh lease of life. That's another reason why I considered it my duty to see you: suppose she did raise the money, and someone murdered her to steal it."

He said a little absently: "It's a possibility we won't overlook, though it's unlikely she would keep such a sum in treasury notes about her person." He consulted a typed sheet on his desk. "If I might ask you one or two questions, Miss Dunston? In 1956 Monica Price was married at the age of twenty-two to Richard Edward Price. Four years later they were divorced. She was the petitioner. Did Mrs Price ever talk about her marriage, mention her ex-husband?"

"Never. I assumed she was a widow, but I make it a firm rule never to pry into people's private affairs."

"She was known to have had a number of male friends. During the period she worked for you, do you remember any particular one? Say telephoning, calling in the shop, perhaps collecting her at closing time?"

Miss Dunston looked affronted. "My assistants were never permitted to have private telephone calls during shop hours. None would have dreamed of gossiping while customers waited to be served. Mrs Price had her own transport, a car she parked at the rear of the premises."

"She spent a good many evenings drinking in public houses, particularly the Pelican, did she . . ."

Miss Dunston permitted herself the discourtesy of interrupting him. "If you're asking did I ever see her the worse for drink, Superintendent, the answer is no. That is another facet of her character that has been wickedly exaggerated."

As evidence that she was about to take her departure, she picked up her handbag, gloves from the desk. "I've told you all I know. My sole reason for coming here was that I wished it placed on official record that Monica Price was neither a drunkard nor an immoral woman."

"In your experience," he said under his breath before he came to his feet. "And I would like to thank you, Miss Dunston. If I need to get in touch with you, may I contact you at the Claremont Hotel?"

"If you wish."

"And if you should recall anything else . . . say a name Mrs Price may have dropped, or any other relevant fact, perhaps you would let me know."

"I will, but it isn't likely. I have an exceptionally reliable memory."

Going towards the door he held open for her, she told herself that the effort she'd made was praiseworthy. Her reward, a clear conscience. But the sense left with her was not the lightness she had anticipated, rather a sense of anticlimax because she was not wholly convinced that Det. Superintendent Ross had accepted as Gospel truth the testimony she'd been at such pains to lay before him.

When he held out his nicotine-stained fingers, the resentment at finding herself undervalued was swamped under the scarcely believable fact of brutal murder committed on a woman to whom she'd served sherry in her father's best crystal glasses.

She said, her normally bell-like voice husky with distress: "It's so long ago, will you be able to find the man who killed her?"

"There's every hope. Good day, Miss Dunston. Thank you for your trouble."

A few minutes before eleven on Sunday morning Ashley pressed his finger on a bell beneath a nickel frame surrounding Tony West's name. Tony's voice, distorted by the speaking tube, came back at him. "Yes. Who is it?"

"Ashley. Let me up."

A longish pause filled by amplified breathing suggesting deliberation preceded the click of the lock release. Walking up to the first floor Ashley speculated on whether he'd caught Tony at breakfast with a girl. But since that had occurred once before, causing no embarrassment to any of the parties concerned, it shouldn't bother him. More likely, he decided, the hesitation was an extension of Tony's recent disinclination to be cornered into a tête-à-tête.

The sale of the six-berth caravan had gone through, but no cock-a-hoop salesman had come breezing into the showroom. On the three occasions on which Ashley had tried to reach him by telephone on Saturday he'd either not been in his office or heavily engaged with a client, which posed a question: Why was the so-called expert on murder studiously avoiding him? A guilty conscience at having overreached himself in the disclosures he'd made to Sergeant Curtis about Ashley Jones? More than likely. But to keep ahead, to prime his wits, Ashley needed to know for certain, be rid of distracting doubt.

Yet, when Tony opened his flat door, the chubby cat-face was wreathed in a welcoming smile. "On the Sabbath! What goes? I always pictured you breakfasting in bed, not tearing yourself away from the dirt in the Sunday papers till gone noon. But enter, early bird." He made a mock salaam.

The flat was commodious for a bachelor, one of four converted out of a Georgian house. Tony, who had signed the lease at the end of his first year with Gasson's, had spared no expense on the furnishing, but he'd run short on taste. Regrettably, colourful opulence was the keynote.

The close-carpeted sitting-room had windows opening on to a balcony with an iron staircase which twisted down into the communal garden. Pulled up to them was a jumbo-sized black leather swivel armchair, a matching foot-rest. On a reproduction Italian marble table handy to his reach stood electric coffee pot, cigarettes, the congealed remains of a cooked breakfast—for one. The floor was awash with news-papers. And lined up in a bookcase behind Tony, something that had hitherto escaped Ashley's eye. A jam-packed row of paper-backed mysteries and who-dun-its; above them heavy tomes in hard-covers, only two titles of which he could read at a distance. *Crime and Criminals; History of English Murder Trials, Vol. 1.*

"Mind if I finish my coffee?" Tony enquired. "Can I offer you a cup?" When Ashley shook his head, Tony waved him to a more modest armchair, stretched out in his own, snuggled into perfect ease, before he asked: "Trouble on the home front?"

Since Tony neglected to offer him a cigarette, Ashley took one from his case. "Why should there be?"

Tony lifted shoulders that were clothed in a short Paisley patterned silk dressing-gown, glanced admiringly at his Turkish-styled house slippers before he answered. "Surely a logical deduction! An old flame gets herself bumped off in decidedly sordid circumstances. Isn't Meg finding it . . . well, just a leetle embarrassing?"

"No more my old flame than yours!"

"Oh, I wouldn't say that," Tony said reproachfully. "Monica cherished a grand passion for you. She told me so once, in her cups of course."

It was a lie, or an artful shot in the dark. Monica had wisely—and wilily—kept her affairs strictly compartmented, never gossiping about one man to another. And he should know! It being pointless to pursue a line of talk that would get him nowhere, he enquired: "What's happening . . . from the police angle, I mean?"

Tony's smile was as mischievously taunting as a child's. "That would be telling."

"I'm asking you to tell me."

Tony pursed his small mouth, announced pompously: "I don't consider at this stage I'd be justified in disclosing confidential information."

Ashley had hard work not to laugh in his face. As if Tony could ever resist publicly exhibiting any mite of superior knowledge! All he had to do was to pretend he didn't want to know, and Tony would break loose. He remarked disinterestedly: "I was under the impression that it had all died down."

"Died down! But, what gave you that idea! A murder hunt never dies. In this one the police have got a dozen irons in the fire, all nicely hotting up. Ross is hell-bent at the moment on finding Monica's car."

Ashley covered the jolt to his nerves by drawing deeply on his cigarette. "Car?" he queried, and exclaimed silently: Not another Act of God!

Tony went on with heavy patience: "Did you ever see Monica out of stilt heels? A three-and-a-half-mile walk! Not quite her, is it? She either drove herself to Dene Valley or someone gave her a lift. So, in either event, what happened to her car?"

"You tell me," Ashley suggested.

Tony ignored the invitation. "They're also after her ex-husband who, rather curiously, hasn't come forward. They were married at Lambeth Registry Office ten years ago. She was twenty-two, the groom, Richard Edward Price, twenty-six. Four years later she divorced him. Most of their married life was spent in a flat in Brixton in a street that was bulldozed out of existence years ago—so no helpful neighbours.

No record either of Richard Edward Price's death, so he's got to be somewhere. Wonder what he's thinking as of this minute." He cocked his head, peered with sly intentness into Ashley's face. "Monica ever mention him to you?"

"No. Where did you get all this dope on him?"

"Little birds," Tony answered airily. "Friendly little birds."

Involuntarily he glanced downwards, and Ashley's glance followed to pick out the Helton Gazette among the National Sunday papers. More precisely one little bird, by name Errol Simpson.

Simpson was senior reporter on the Helton Gazette, an inebriated cynic, willing to sell any information to which he was privy for the price of a double brandy. Ashley suffered a spasm of irritation that it hadn't crossed his mind to beat Tony in tapping that valuable source himself.

Tony said with lightly veiled zest: "Do I detect signs that we are, despite our protestations to the contrary, just a wee bit rattled?"

"I don't get you. I've got a clean sheet with the police."

Tony threw back his head in a loud chortling laugh. "You innocent! All you've suffered is the first round: routine enquiries by a sergeant. You've got the higher echelons of the police ahead of you, particularly Ross." He mimicked: "Are you quite sure, Mr Jones, that you can't recall the last occasion on which you saw Monica Price?"

Ashley swore under his breath. "Who can, after two years?"

Tony looked smug. "Me, for one. The house-warming party I gave in this flat, two weeks after I moved in, that's why I can give you the date. Saturday, May fifteenth. Generously entertained all me old chums. I'd just banked my first big commission cheque from Gasson's, so it was lavish and wild. Monica was here, though not in her best form because you'd, a little callously I thought, brought Meg along. Libby, too, if my memory serves me right, wasn't exactly a ball of fire. It must have been on that night that she finally got the message: Meg had won. You and Meg slunk off early, so maybe you didn't take much account of the broken hearts you left scattered on the carpet."

Ashley forced a grin. "Dead and buried. I don't remember seeing Monica, but if you say she was there . . ."

Tony murmured: "More precisely, dead but not buried deeply enough." His little round eyes flicked at Ashley for a reaction before he went on: "Actually, the party wasn't the last time I saw Monica. That was on Saturday, May twenty-ninth. Again, most fortunately, on record, as it was the day after my membership of the Helton Golf Club had been accepted, and I was on my way to buy my first round of drinks at the bar. I got caught behind that old rattletrap of hers at the traffic lights at the top of the High Street. Naturally, on the green, she stalled, and I got ahead of her. I waved, but she was too burned up to notice me. Funny to think the last sight I had of poor old Monica was in a rear mirror." He sighed, added pompously: "Little did I realise its significance!"

"Significance?"

"It turns out that, to date, bar whoever murdered her, I was the last person to see her alive. Key witness! Mrs Warren can't remember whether Monica went back to her room that night, but she's positive she'd vanished by Monday morning. She could conceivably have been alive after Sunday, but until they've got proof, the police have marked a bloody great ring round Sunday, May thirtieth. How's your alibi?"

"Good grief, how's anybody's. I haven't a clue in hell where I was, what I was doing."

"Ask Meg," Tony suggested. "Engaged, or on the brink.

Maybe she's got it all written up in a diary tied up in pink ribbon."

"Meg doesn't keep a diary."

"Hard luck." Tony brushed a speck of ash from his sleeve. "By the way Ian rang last night. Apparently they're throwing a party next Saturday. You know, in the end, Libby didn't do too badly for herself. Not much money, of course, but in his own thick way Ian dotes on her. Of course, he bores the pants off her, but that's life, you never get everything. You and Meg going?"

Ashley's hand had been forced by a chance encounter between Meg and Libby on Saturday morning. Meg had reproached him: "Darling, you never told me about Libby's party. She says she asked you to. Don't you want to go?"

Undecided because his subconscious still hadn't reproduced the dream, he had cynically thrown the decision at Meg—mentally tossed a coin. There'd been earnest and boring deliberation. Now she could. Now she couldn't. The keystone and the decision had proved to be Sister Melton. Would she be willing to baby-sit for Pip and the Red Man? It turned out she would, subject to the proviso of an emergency call. More shilly-shallying before Meg worked out that, if the worst happened, Sister Melton could telephone her at Libby's and she would dive into her car. The maximum time the Red Man and Pip would be left untended would be eight minutes. They would go.

"We'll be there. What about you?"

"Why not. Ian's a generous host." Tony jabbed out his cigarette. "Ashley, old man, I feel a swine pushing you out, but you did take me on the hop, and I've got a date at twelve."

Ashley left, taking with him confirmation of Tony's addiction to crime in fact and fiction, a hard suspicion that he was buying drinks for Errol Simpson in exchange for scraps of information gleaned from police headquarters, but what else? Nothing of which to be absolutely sure.

He stopped at a newsagent's to buy two of the more sensational Sunday newspapers that weren't allowed to defile the letter-box of Laburnum Lodge, and then, on impulse, made a short detour that took him past Helton Police station. Pulling into a convenient parking slot a couple of hundred yards ahead on the opposite side of the street, he altered the angle of his rear mirror to give him a view of the singularly unimpressive building: red brick begrimed with fifty years' accumulation of soot, smudged windows, scabby paint, it looked more like a receiving station for drunks and disorderlies, perpetrators of petty crime, than the nerve-centre of a highly mechanised, computer-operated murder hunt.

The sound of cars being gunned into action in the underground park at the rear interrupted a reverie that was comfortably unalarmed. Two halted at the entrance, drivers leaping out to open doors for five male passengers. In the second that they were level with him Ashley recognised Sergeant Curtis; the remaining four were another plain-clothes officer of his ilk, plus three more substantially built, older men. Which, he wondered, was Tony's hero, Ross? He was in time at the crossroads to see one car take a route that would lead it to Crumley or any one of half a dozen villages. Past the restriction sign the car put on speed, and he made no attempt to catch it up. Instead he pulled into a lay-by, began his examination of the two newspapers that assumed their readers would be enthralled by a detailed recap of every relevant and irrelevant item touching on the Reservoir Murder.

Search for Murder Victim's Missing Car. Police Seek Murdered Girl's Ex-Husband, they screamed. Mrs Warren had made a statement; so had the woman with a room above the one Monica had occupied, the landlord of the Pelican Inn, several so-called friends of the dead woman, ambitious to read their names in print. His wasn't among them; neither was Tony's. All he read confirmed what he'd suspected: Tony had disclosed to him no fact other than the details of Monica's marriage he would have got from Errol Simpson that he couldn't have discovered for himself. Just a compulsive show-off!

Reassured, his eye was caught by a headline on the lower half of the page. "Housewife's Miracle Escape." He read on. With hands dripping water, a woman in Nottingham had filled a plugged-in faulty electric kettle while standing on a wet floor. But for the prompt action of her husband who'd administered the kiss of life, the result would have been fatal.

The Red Man's nobility was restricted to head, arms, hands. Twice within the last year there'd been an unholy rumpus in the night when he'd knocked over his bedside cabinet while struggling to switch on his bed-light. A faulty electrical connection? Insufficient power for a lethal result.

His glance flew wider for inspiration. A twenty-year-old student had died from gas poisoning due to a slow leak in a pipe joint. No gas at Laburnum Lodge. A toddler had been found drowned in a twelve-foot-deep garden pond. A woman had been charged with the murder of her husband by deliberately running him down in a cul-de-sac.

Both methods pre-supposed a victim able to stand up and walk. The Red Man was a solid hulk tied to his bed. A ten-year-old boy could have smothered him. Smother . . . the word triggered off a tantalising image of the Red Man, already stifled, tipped out of bed into a cunningly contrived heap of pillows on which he would appear to have suffocated. But the Red Man had never fallen out of bed; couldn't because he was anchored there by his dead legs.

What about the upper half of his body, thrust over the edge, left there . . . In such a posture, with a little preliminary doctoring, wouldn't he choke to death?

Minute as the spark was, it gave him a boost. Work on it . . . and he might arrive at a practical scheme. Considering the times the Red Man came near to choking on his own spleen, the idea contained an element of poetic justice he found richly diverting.

A mile outside Crumley on the Helton Road was the private drive that led to the Thomas's farm, emblazoned with a sign Ian all but saluted each time he went in or out. BEECHGROVE PEDIGREE JERSEY HERD. Automatically Ashley's glance swung up it. Sometimes he'd catch a glimpse of Prince if he were loose.

Today, even if the dog had been out, any view of him would have been blocked by the police car waiting to leave the drive, cross the line of traffic into the main road. As soon as he was by, it was on his heels.

Keeping his speed down to the regulation forty, Ashley flicked on his indicator to signal his right-turn, experiencing not fear, but a revving up of his thought processes in preparation for what might lie ahead if the car followed. But when he turned into Laburnum Lodge, it passed on his near side.

A good omen! Despite Tony's typical malice in predicting otherwise, the police, he decided, had ticked him off their list of suspects.

When he'd garaged the car, all he had pressing on his mind was the disposal of the Red Man—and faintly, on the farthest horizon of consciousness, scarcely visible, the speculation that had reared out of the night at him. If he hadn't killed Monica, was her murderer someone he knew—or someone who knew him?

Chapter 6

From boyhood Frederick Gasson had been a dedicated early riser. By his reckoning the best part of the day was spent before most people rubbed the sleep out of their eyes. Fate could have designed no crueler life-sentence than to imprison him on a bed. By five to nine on Monday morning when, through the open window, he saw Ashley stroll like a member of the landed gentry towards the garage, he had been fed, blanket-bathed and dosed.

Watching Hexham tidy up, he ruminated idly on why an able-bodied young man should choose to earn his livelihood by playing nurse-lackey to the chronically sick. He'd never been sufficiently curious to enquire; Hexham served him well enough: not one to chatter inanities, he wasn't averse to giving him a straight answer to a straight question, which came in useful on occasions.

"Pass me my glasses," he ordered, "and the paper. Hodkins is due at eleven. Ask Mrs Jones for a bottle of Tio Pepe and two glasses. Once you've shown him in, you can make yourself scarce for an hour."

Brian Hodkins was the new young solicitor he'd been at pains to acquire after he'd fired old Barclay a month ago. Past it, he'd been, as empty of ideas as he was himself of how to nail up Meg's inheritance so that Ashley wouldn't be able to get his thieving hands on more than the interest. The Gordian knot, as Barclay had wearisomely reiterated, was the sizable blocks of property and land in Helton that Frederick had, with acumen and foresight, acquired over the years in preparation for the day when the centre of the town came under development. Sell it now, forfeit his rightful profit, put the money in trust for Meg and Pip, or hang on, knowing that if he died before it was sold, the capital sum Meg received would be filched from her. The same insoluble query lay over the Crumley garage. He could will it to Meg all right, but Ashley would have cajoled her into selling it, pocketed the proceeds, before he was cold in his grave. Sell it now? He groaned. The other alternative, a partner, or partners, was equally unpalatable. Give a man, even a good man, like Tom Norris, an ounce of power, a pinch of authority and you ran the risk that overnight he'd step out of line, start dictating to you. Besides, running the only business he'd retained after his accident was the life-belt that hauled him out of his pitch-black days. If only he knew how long he'd got.

"You could live to be a hundred," was all that fool Pratt would commit himself to, "as long as you ration yourself to one bout of temper a week."

As if he wanted another forty-four years tethered to a bed! Dispassionately he asked himself if he'd mind dying tomorrow, and gave himself a truthful answer. Not if he could be sure that Ashley Jones wouldn't enjoy a spendthrift, idle existence on money that he'd sweated to earn; desert Meg for another woman as soon as he'd squandered her capital.

How could a daughter of his remain so wilfully blind, clamp herself in blinkers! Presented with a list of the fly-by-nights who'd been her future husband's familiars, she'd replied as calmly as if she'd been the one preaching reason: "They belong to the past, Daddy. When Ashley was friendly with them, he didn't know me. It's different now. We're going to be married."

God save her, he muttered fervently. Now this murder. A common tart, whose name had been on the list he'd paid Dodge to lay before Meg. If he'd had a hand in it, if the police caught up with him . . . The prospect of revenge was sweet, but in a second it went sour on his tongue. Meg's husband in prison for life, his grandson's father a gaolbird!

Sometimes it seemed that he'd only be released from the rack if Ashley fell under a bus. At others, in the stupefying ordeal of the nights when he couldn't sleep, if he could get his hands on a gun, blast it through Ashley Jones's heart.

And he had a gun, a Luger 9-mm. automatic pistol, tucked away at the back of the bottom left-hand drawer of the sideboard in the dining-room, a souvenir of the Second World War he'd bought from Sam Goodsell, when he'd been hard up. Ammunition, too. But packed in a stout wooden box, tied up with cord. Send Hexham to bring it to him, lay it on the bed. At that point hope died. He hadn't sufficient strength in his fingers to untie the cord, open the box, let alone load the pistol. And if he got someone to do it for him, Meg would hear about it, make short work of confiscating the box and its contents.

From Mr Gasson's bathroom window Hexham watched the Jaguar turn into the main road. By the time the sound of the engine had died on the air his mouth had lost its tight line and his body had assumed a slightly more relaxed pose. The exit of Ashley Jones from the house had the same effect on him as the removal of an oppressive weight.

Or was that no more than a neurosis that he deliberately encouraged by persuading himself that intuition, eyes he believed were keener and had less to distract them than other people's, provided him with sound evidence for what he wanted to believe? Sometimes he wondered whether it was all a fandango of baseless prejudice. But mostly he was sure that his dark conviction was valid.

A letter that had arrived by the morning's post from his mother in Croydon was tucked into the pocket of his white coat, its contents read at lightning speed because they had been wholly predictable. A wailing wall of hand-written lament over the bright and prosperous future stolen from her by the unforgivable wickedness of her only surviving child. He had written he would be with her by tea-time on Saturday, leave on Sunday evening. She complained bitterly that the visit was too short . . . and yet by the end of half an hour in his company, she would not be able to endure the sight of his face.

The new ground-floor wing backed on to the kitchen. By standing with his ear close to the bathroom wall, he could hear the murmur of Meg's voice scolding Pip, then, a second later, a carol of laughter. He did not budge until they moved into the garden, out of earshot.

It was one of Mrs Wisley's little eccentricities to arrange the post pyramidwise, largest sheets at the base, slanting upwards symmetrically to an apex of notes, postcards. On Monday morning the topmost item was a cheap manilla envelope inscribed in under-scored block letters at the left-hand corner: *Personal and Confidential*. Assuming it was some piffling, forgotten debt that had caught up with him, Ashley laid it aside to open last. When he did so, what fell out was not a letter but a white ruled filing card on which were printed three lines of block capitals.

SO YOUR KEEP NET
HAD A HOLE IN IT
AND THE FISH GOT AWAY!

His reaction was similar to that of a man who, thinking he has come to the bottom of a flight of stairs, discovers, too late, there is one more, and for an alarming instant is suspended in space before he regains his foothold. Back on balance he retrieved the envelope he had tossed into the waste basket. Posted in Crumley yesterday afternoon.

So what in hell did it amount to: Joke or threat? Whichever it was, it had been written by someone who with a childlike attempt at humour had contrived an inane play on words. Keeper's Cottage. Keep net—the spiral net which fishermen hung in water to keep their catch fresh until it was packed in a creel to carry home. But there, he thought savagely, they'd fallen down. Monica hadn't been going anywhere.

He scanned the lines minutely for signs of an overt threat, any inference of it being the opening move in a game of blackmail? What cards did the writer hold up his sleeve. None. All England knew Monica's bones had been unearthed in Keeper's Cottage. His earlier association with her, though not perhaps its degree, had been common knowledge, so suspicion pinned on him could apply to four, five, maybe more, other men.

On balance he was inclined to define the card as an essay in malicious humour, intended to jangle his nerves. It followed automatically that it had been penned by one of the Red Man's spies whose ultimate ambition it was to dig a pit beneath his feet.

He lined them up; Tony, Mrs Wisley, Tom Norris, Sam Goodsell, Hexham. First the fishing clue. Goodsell and Tom Norris went coarse fishing in the winter. Mrs Wisley didn't, but her husband, Ashley happened to know, was a member of Helton Anglers' Club. Tony? A smattering of the parlance of every sport, along with the departure times of car-ferries to the Continent, the addresses of camping sites, airy references to the bliss of carefree open-air living, were part and parcel of his sales talk to clients. Hexham? God only knew whether Hexham was a fisherman. He could have been the all-England boy-champion angler for all he . . .

From nowhere came a blast of fearsome speculation: was it remotely feasible that for all his infinity of pains, some creeping spy had seen him near Keeper's Cottage that Sunday? It was not: the card was no more than a wild shot in the dark designed to rob him of sleep at night.

He had been so deeply absorbed in assessing the motive behind the stupid jibe that he had been rendered momentarily deaf. Mrs Wisley, without audible warning, had entered the gold-fish bowl, was planted in front of his desk, striving to read the card upside down. Automatically he spread his fingers to block her view, looked up to catch the expression in her round toffee-brown eyes. Even more smug than usual. Preening herself that a paper dart had struck home?

"There's another policeman to see you, Mr Jones. A Superintendent this time. Very important, I believe. Detective Superintendent Ross from the County Police. Shall I show him in?"

"Yes, of course." As she turned, Ashley slid the card and envelope under a sales brochure. Over her shoulder he gained an impression of a thick-set, middle-aged man, with sparse, ill-combed grey hair, ambling round the showroom, pausing at random to run an eye over a display model. Not a man under pressure, not a man anticipating exerting it on someone else. A figure that in no way matched up to the ruthless super-sleuth Tony had set up on a pedestal for him to revere.

The impression lasted while Ross shook hands, seated himself, accepted a cigarette. It was only when Ashley bent forward to give him a light that he felt the impact of a narrowed glance so direct and probing that he had a sense of looking into a camera lens that was busy recording not only his physical image but the thoughts buried in his head. He blinked once, decided that it was an extremely unpleasant face, thin, sharp features covered in yellowy skin, at odds with the rotund body.

Yet when Ross began to speak, there was no actual hostility in his slightly abrupt voice. "Mr Jones, I've read a report of the information on Monica Price you were kind enough to give Sergeant Curtis on Friday. Since then there have been one or two developments, which is why I'm here, in the hope that you may be able to amplify your statement to him."

Ashley's smile was one of pleasure at receiving good news. "Developments! That means you're on the track of the murderer?"

"Let's say we've built up a clear picture of Monica Price's movements up to the day she was murdered."

"You actually know the date! That's a smart piece of deduction, isn't it, when she's been dead over a couple of years?"

Ross made a vague gesture of disclaimer. "We have a witness who saw her driving down the High Street on the evening of Saturday the 29th May. The woman who still occupies the room above the one Monica Price rented, though she didn't actually see her, is quite definite that she heard her come home late on Saturday night, leave around lunchtime on Sunday. A youth who was in the habit of parking his scooter behind her car in Farrow's Lane is positive it wasn't there when he went out at 2 o'clock. He remembers the occasion because she had borrowed half-a-crown from him the day before, and he wanted to ask her to repay it. He never saw her or the car again. Therefore, until we have any contradictory evidence, it is a reasonable assumption that Monica Price was murdered during Sunday, May 30th or in the early hours of Monday morning."

"I see." Ashley moved his head in good-humoured bewilderment. "But what I don't see, I'm afraid, is where I come in."

"Like this. It is our experience that when people have had time to consider at leisure events that took place some time ago, their memories sharpen. Trivial incidents, of seemingly no acount, so naturally forgotten, tend to re-emerge. I am wondering if that is so in your case, Mr Jones. If there is anything you can add to your statement to Sergeant Curtis."

"Sorry, Superintendent. Not a thing."

If Ross had suffered any disappointment, he did not voice it. Instead he left a patch of silence during which he appeared to be taking a series of snapshots of the gold-fish bowl. When it was beginning to drag on Ashley's nerves, he brought it to an abrupt end. "Mr Jones, I believe during the period in which we are interested, you rented a room at No. 10, Prince of Wales's Terrace, were employed by the Helton Mutual Benefits Society as an insurance salesman?"

"That is correct."

"Which post you left to take over the management of this business. What date was that, Mr Jones?"

"I don't remember the exact day. It's on record, of course. I could have it looked up. At a guess, I'd say about the beginning of July."

"After your marriage to Margaret Gasson?"

"A few days, possibly a week."

"And the date of your wedding was?"

For the life of him he couldn't remember. The last Saturday in June, the first in July? To cover the bound of panic, he forced a comic laugh of dismay. "There you have me, Superintendent. Most reprehensibly my wife always has to remind me. I think it was the last Saturday in June."

"You didn't go away for a honeymoon?"

Ashley permitted himself a hint of irony. "No. As I expect you know, my wife has an invalid father. It ties her to the house. For the same reason our engagement was a short one, the wedding what is termed 'quiet.'"

"Actually, I once met your father-in-law, but it was a good few years ago. I was a detective-sergeant investigating the theft of his car, which happily was recovered. He's completely bedridden since his accident, is he?"

"I'm afraid so." Ashley found the idea of any link, however tenuous, between the police and the Red Man repugnant.

Ross's creased, yellowy lid parted a fraction wider, and he said with heightening of the verbal pressure: "Mr Jones, one of the luxuries a policeman on a murder hunt can't afford is tact. No time for it. Were you at any time on terms of sexual intimacy with Monica Price?"

"No."

"Can you give me the name of any man whom you know to have been her lover?"

"No."

"Could you hazard a guess, Mr Jones?"

"No." He smiled reproachfully. "In doing so I might be as way off course as the informant who gave my name to you."

Again there followed a long-drawn-out pause suggesting that Ross was in command of the interview, under no compulsion to keep the oil of conversation flowing. He stared so long at the filing cabinet that Ashley was driven to say: "Look, Superintendent, I'm anxious to help . . ."

"Mr Jones, did Monica Price ever try to borrow money from you?"

"I told your sergeant . . ."

"I don't mean the odd fiver over a drink, I mean a substantial sum, some hundreds of pounds, even more?"

"She'd know better than to waste her breath. In those days I hadn't a bean." When Ross made no comment, he added with pardonable irritation, "You must be aware of that from the enquiries you've made."

"But you had prospects, Mr Jones."

"Not that high. Since it interests you, Superintendent, I am not even at this moment in a position to act as banker to the tune of one hundred pounds, let alone several. My bank manager will verify this if you ask him."

"Can you suggest anyone among Monica Price's acquaintances whom she might have approached in the hope of obtaining a substantial loan?"

"Not with a chance of getting it. Tony West . . ." He shook his head. "He had more money than most of us, but I wouldn't say any to spare. Do you know Monica was trying to borrow money?"

"We have reason to suspect she was. Now, Mr Jones, at the risk of being repetitious, can you remember when you last saw Monica Price?"

"I've already explained to your sergeant . . ." Then memory tugged, and he smiled apologetically. "Yes, actually, Superintendent, I am able to help you a bit there. Since I saw Sergeant Curtis on Friday, I've learned from Tony West that Monica was at his house-warming party on May 15th. I escorted the girl who was about to become my fiancée. I've no recollection of seeing Monica, but if Tony says she was there . . . well probably I did, but I certainly didn't speak to her. It was a very large and crowded party!"

Ross made a half movement as if he was on the point of rising, then changed his mind. "What car were you driving two years ago?"

"A company car. Morris 1100. They were standard issue to salesmen."

"Colour?"

"Dark green."

"Registration number?"

"Sorry, it's gone out of my head. Helton Mutual Benefits Society will have it on record. How's the number of my car going to help you?"

"We have reports of a number of cars near the reservoir during that particular weekend."

Ashley exclaimed in disbelief: "After all this time!"

"You'd be surprised the odd details people come up with when they're asked to think hard."

"Not me. Anyway, I never went near the reservoir."

"If you're certain, a negative is just as useful."

This time he did rise. His expression of thanks for the interview was so neutral that Ashley was left without a clue as to whether he counted his time wasted or well spent, whether he was saying goodbye or au revoir.

As he sat down Ashley found himself expelling his breath as though he'd been under a compulsion to hold it longer than was comfortable. The money! It had been a shock to learn that the police had discovered from some source— probably the old woman who owned the shop—that Monica had been trying to raise it. The pulse-beats of alarm mounted, then slowed down, died. Without evidence laid by a dead tongue, how could they ever find out that Monica had picked him as her private gold mine? The answer was that they couldn't.

With a flinch of repugnance, he slid the card and envelope out from its hiding place. Directing a cautious glance towards Mrs Wisley's desk, he found Tom Norris closeted with her, their mouths opening and shutting in a tableau of intimacy that nauseated him.

Had that unholy alliance worked in unison, cooked up that ridiculous taunting jingle between them? Sniggered, heads together as they were now, over a kids' trick to put the wind up him?

Or Tony, committing to writing the sly innuendoes of his normal conversational exchange? Or Sam Goodsell, who only held his job by the Red Man's patronage, printing in block letters while he hee-heed to himself?

Or Hexham? Because Hexham, he knew in his bones, hated him, not with the contemptuous ill will of the other four, avid to see him fall from grace, but with a detestation that matched his own. Hexham, vindictively shaking a fist in his face?

The effort required to set the four men, one woman in a line, weigh their potential for malice, drove him to an unbearable pitch of frustration. Release came only by bringing speculation to an abrupt end. Instead concentrate on the act that would line his pockets for ever more. It was midday on Monday with only five clear days between him and a deadline when he must have set out in his head a detailed time-table of the Red Man's last hour on earth.

Chapter 7

Ferncliffe Private Hotel, though not sited in the fashionable
end of Redley Bay, did provide a view of the sea from its
attic windows, an asset that had paid off handsomely in the
hottest summer for a quarter of a century. Valerie Toombs,
laying tables for breakfast in the basement dining-room,
thought if the roof had been flat they could have set beds
up there, raked in more lolly. Every limb in her body had a
separate and distinct ache, her feet screamed a protest each
time she put them to the ground, but her spirit was as
buoyant as a bird's: there was a good chance, come Septem-
ber 25th, that they'd be in the black instead of the red. No
crippling debts! It was a state of bliss beyond the scope of
her imagination.

She wiped back a fringe that was mouse except at its
metallic tips for lack of an hour to escape to a hairdresser,
rubbed the small of her back above a waist that had shrunk
two inches since May . . . at forty-eight she couldn't afford
to get any skinnier, looked at her watch. Nearly midnight
and half the guests still out. Well, Les would have to sit up,
lock the front door at 12.30. She was no more use than a
walking zombie.

She dragged herself to the cubby-hole under the stairs

which bore the legend "Office," collapsed into a chair. Les threw her a wink, but the most she could give him in return was a wan grin. "I was going up to bed, but now I'm sat down, I'm not sure I'll be able to stagger up again."

"If you wait until I've written out the last few bills, I'll fix us a drink. Then up with you. I'll cope with the night's merrymakers."

"I certainly couldn't. They can sleep on the beach for all I care." She pulled towards her the newspaper she'd studied off and on all day. "Les, I still feel we ought to go to the police. It's her, not a doubt."

A short man in his late fifties, with a hang-dog face, who for eight years had been nursing the ulcer that had forced him into what was supposedly a sedentary job, he burst into vehemence, rare in him. "Now, Val, we've been all over that, and the answer's still no. She's been dead and buried for two years. We can't do her any good, can we!"

"Not her, I grant you. But if a murderer gets away with it once, they say he'll try it again."

Flushing with exasperation he thrust the bill into an envelope. "You want the police here, nosing around. Coppers in uniform arriving while we're serving lunch! Families with kids, they're our bread and butter, and they're not the sort to get a kick out of falling over a policeman on the stairs."

"But, Les, *we* haven't done anything."

"Leaves all the more scope for a few nice sensational rumours. Before we've had time to turn round, it'll be all over town that I've been peddling purple hearts. No, Val, it's not on. We're going to keep our noses clean."

She said stubbornly: "I looked up the date. July, three years ago. Two nights, Saturday and Sunday. Mr and Mrs Price. Just London scrawled for an address. And it's him they're after."

"To help with their enquiries, which is their way of saying they suspect he bumped her off! Sightseers staring in at the windows, trying to decide which room they slept in! You must be out of your mind."

"But, Les, if it was him . . ."

"For God's sake," he bawled, "we don't even know he was her husband."

"He must have been. If you skip off for a sly weekend, you either sign the man's name or pick a new one. I never heard of a couple registering under the girl's name. Did you? And it was her, Les. I'm positive."

Without a word he went out, returned after a couple of minutes with two generous whiskies on a tray, and his temper under control. "Now, Val, it's time you looked two simple facts in the face. One, admit we've had more than our fair share of bad luck. Well, we have, haven't we?"

She nodded.

"And, two, when for the first time in ten years we can see a patch of blue sky ahead, we'd be crazy to go begging for more. Right?"

She nodded again.

"So it follows, forget Monica Price. She's certainly rid of her troubles, and let's you and me drink to a dozen hot summers in a row. By that time we'll have our feet up in someone else's hotel, with them waiting on us. Okay, no more talking of running to the police?"

"Okay," she murmured as she lifted her glass. "But I still think we ought to. I've got a conscience about murderers, particularly those who've got off scot free for two years."

Occasionally the treadmill of Frederick Gasson's existence was relieved by the arrival of the afternoon post. If Meg wasn't around, provided he caught sight of the post van arriving, he could dispatch Hexham to get it out of the box, bring it to him. Sorting it himself, instead of having his portion doled out to him, gave him the delusion that he was still master in his own house.

This happened on Tuesday afternoon when he was harassed beyond mortal bearing. Just before lunch a car had driven up, and a man whom he'd recognised as a middle-aged version of the detective sergeant he'd known years before, had got out, asked Elsie when she answered the door, for Meg.

Det. Superintendent Ross, who, so Mrs Wisley informed him, had been closeted with Ashley for the best part of an hour on Monday morning, by-passing him in his search for a murderer to catechise his daughter. Twenty minutes he'd spent with her, and when, after he'd left, Frederick had tackled Meg, charged her with not bringing Ross to his bedside, she'd dismissed the matter with as little concern as if Ross had been the vicar come to plead for a donation to his Church Repair Fund. "It was a routine call, Daddy. They're visiting everyone."

"So I hear. He spent an hour with Ashley yesterday."

"Yes," she said, but she'd blinked in surprise and he'd known she'd lied. As if Ashley would be likely to tell her!

"Then why don't they come to see me. Why am I left out?"

"Why on earth should the police worry you! When she was murdered you'd been ill in bed for nearly a year."

And all this while he was still labouring under the crushing disappointment left behind by young Hodkins' failure to produce a miracle scheme to frustrate his son-in-law's avarice. All he'd done had been to repeat Barclay's dreary advice: Sell his capital assets, invest the proceeds in Trusts for Meg and Pip . . . plus an original footnote that Barclay had never dared to utter: "There is no means, I'm afraid, by which we can impose restriction on Mrs Jones as to how she spends the interest accruing from the substantial trusts set up for her and your grandson." In other words, sell or hold, and Ashley would still live like a lord on his money.

For the first time, he found himself regretting the wealth he'd sweated to pile up; without it Meg would have been safe . . . though if she'd been poor Ashley Jones would never have married her! His lips emitting the grunt that was the only outward evidence of the grim battle that was perpetually waging inside him, he ordered Hexham to fetch the post.

Not much of a bag. A couple of soap coupons for Meg, her bank statement. He toyed with the notion of opening it, thought better of the idea. Certain trivial liberties had a way of so affronting her that she aired her displeasure by ignoring him for days . . . keeping Pip out of his sight. A letter from his sister Myra. A bill from the plumber grossly overcharging for fixing a couple of washers. Daylight robbery!

It was on this burst of righteous indignation that he turned to the last envelope. Ashley Jones, Esq., printed in block capitals, above it, underlined: Personal and Confidential. Cheap bill envelope. Smudged, illegible postmark. He explored it delicately with fingertips that had been hard and calloused but were now as sensitive as a woman's. He held it up to the light. More like a card inside than the folded sheet of a letter. Turning it over, he inserted an exploratory fingernail into the sealing. Fast, no chance of prising it open, sticking it down again. He laid it on the bedside table, balancing the satisfaction of opening and destroying it against that of presenting it to Ashley with a demand to know what was inside. Personal and Confidential! A woman dunning him for child maintenance, or an advertisement touting pornographic filth. Could be either, or something worse. When Hexham brought in his tea the envelope lay face down on his bedside cabinet, the decision unmade of how to use it in the war against Ashley Jones that wouldn't end until one of them was dead.

When Ashley drove into the garage on Tuesday evening Meg was waiting for him, pressed against the shelves set into the rear wall. Her presence was a warning light that she considered it imperative she have a quiet word with him before he got inside the house, came face to face with the Red Man. As he braked she slipped into the car, sat close to him.

He kissed her cheek. "What's up?"

"Nothing." She smiled at the warmth that automatically flooded through her when they were reunited after even the shortest of separations. And his calm, that imperious gloss of confidence that was surely his most precious birthright, eased the tight constraint in which she was caught. Why did she fret so unendingly, get thrown into mindless fits of panic at the smallest deviation from normal? Ashley never did. In a flash of insight she saw spread out her shining good fortune. Ashley, Pip, the fulfilment of her duty towards her father whom she could never bring herself to desert.

"Nothing," she repeated. "I'm so glad you're home. I wanted to see you quickly."

He tweaked her ear. "A pretty tale, but there is something, isn't there?"

She gulped down the last of her silly fright. "All right, I wanted to talk to you before you see Daddy. A policeman called this morning . . . well, not an ordinary policeman, not Sergeant Trent, one in plain clothes, Detective Superintendent Ross. Daddy says he was in the office yesterday seeing you, but you never told me."

"Because there was nothing to tell. Anyone who as much

as said hello to Monica is getting a succession of visits from the police. But why on earth did Ross want to see you?"

"Honestly, I don't know. It seemed a waste of his time. Just a chat about this and that. When he'd gone and I went over what he'd asked, all I could think of was that he'd wanted to know when we were married, how long we'd been engaged, where we'd met. Ashley, why should he be interested, question both of us, as if anything about us can have the remotest connection with a woman who was murdered two years ago." She shivered, then burst into passion: "I hate it. Hate it."

He said soothingly: "Policemen carry notebooks, and they have to fill them up with something. Maybe they get a black mark when they get back to headquarters if the pages are blank. So they get busy, ask questions, write down the answers, even if they're meaningless. Darling, I keep telling you, but you won't listen, that there's nothing for you to worry about. Did he go in to see your father?"

"No . . . thank heaven he didn't. I was terrified he'd ask if he could. But Daddy saw the car, heard him ask for me. When I went in afterwards, he was in a terrible state, wanting to know why Ross had come, what he'd asked me."

"And what did you tell him?"

"As little as I could get away with, practically nothing. Apparently, years ago, he knew Ross when he was a young policeman, so he felt snubbed because Ross didn't ask for him, and that made him boil all the more." She beat her clenched fist against her forehead. "I know I'm being unreasonable, they have to do their job, but I can't bear it, all this poking and prying into what concerns no one but you and me. Don't you hate it?" She lifted her head in enquiry, answered herself with a choked, wondering laugh. "You don't, do you? Darling, you're marvellous, you couldn't care less, could you? You take it all in your stride."

If he wasn't worried, he was immensely, unendingly curious, maddeningly exasperated because by a hideous coincidence the past had risen to badger him at the precise moment when he needed his wits unencumbered, at their brightest. At much too frequent intervals for comfort he was piqued by the card and envelope tucked inside his breast pocket, reacting to it as if it were a heckler pestering him with an absurd and totally irrelevant question.

Meg slid her arm under his elbow. "Darling, what I wanted to ask you is . . . well, if Daddy flies into one of his mad rages about the police coming to the house, please don't answer back . . . no matter how he shouts and raves. Otherwise he'll only make himself ill. Sometimes I'm worried that he'll give himself a stroke, die in one of his ghastly fits of temper."

Ashley promised, automatically examining the possibilities of the Red Man's death by a species of inner combustion. Suppose he confessed to a misdemeanour so heinous and unforgivable that the Red Man's response was literally to blast himself off the earth? Say, for instance: "I'm not absolutely sure, but it's on the cards that your beloved only daughter is married to a murderer. . . ." The snag was he couldn't count on the shock proving fatal.

For all the interest the Red Man showed in the day's reports they might have been a wad of blotting paper. Without even glancing at the totals, he fixed his eyes on Ashley, punched an indictment out of his lungs. "Not content with visiting you yesterday morning, the police were here today asking Meg questions about that harlot who got herself murdered. Having your wife grilled by a Detective Superintendent, doesn't that take the smile off your face."

Ashley put on his amiable expression. "I don't see why it should. Naturally, I'm sorry if Meg was upset, but I don't see why she should be. The police are questioning everyone for miles around. It's their duty, isn't it?"

"You're a bit different from everyone else, aren't you? You went to bed with her!"

"Only according to the gospel of Mr Dodge, presumably because the more incriminating he made the lies you hired him to file on me, the more you paid him."

Frederick's eyes bulged with the effort needed to avoid being tricked down a blind alley of dead arguments, concentrate on the present. "Don't make the mistake of underestimating Ross. He's smart. If you as much as knew that woman of yours had been murdered, he'll get you, and with my blessing."

With soft flaying sarcasm, Ashley murmured: "Add mine. He's welcome to work his guts out for all the good it will do him . . . or you," and had the satisfaction of seeing the Red Man's face suffuse with choler until it became the colour of brick-dust, as he made clumsy, crablike exertions to reach an envelope on his bedside cabinet.

The Red Man's voice came forth in a stifled roar. "And what about this? Who's it from? Some pregnant girl blackmailing you!"

Across the three feet of space between him and the Red Man's fist, the block letters zoomed at Ashley. He had to restrain himself from snatching the envelope out of the fish-white grasp. That the anonymous jokesmith had dared to send a second card to his home, with the risk of it being seen by the Red Man or Meg, carried a whisper of menace that set him tingling with shock.

With an elaborately casual gesture he took possession of the envelope, slid his fingers over the reverse side to make sure that it had not been violated.

"Confidential!" he exclaimed in mock reproach. "Personal!"

The two words were sufficient to wreck the Red Man's last bastion of control. Smiling disdain, Ashley stood mute, unperturbed, watching the convulsion work its way through the dead trunk, fight for expression in wildly flailing arms, strangulated grunts.

He only turned his back on the entertainment when his view of the star was blocked by the white-coated nurse-guard. In the hall he collided with Meg.

"What happened? Ashley, let me go to him."

His grasp, smartly reversing her was too firm to permit escape. "No, Hexham's coping, giving him a pill or an injection. I'm the one in need of a drink."

She obeyed, but half-heartedly, her face elongated with the painful division in her loyalties. As she lifted the whisky decanter, Pip's wail floated down the stairs.

"I'll have to go up to him. It's his teeth, they're bothering him terribly, poor mite."

He poured his own whisky, and only after he'd drunk it, poured a second, did he extract the envelope he'd thrust into his pocket. Same card, same block print, same Crumley post-mark, same inane play on words:

SO DEAD GIRLS CAN'T KEEP SECRETS
MAYBE SHE'LL WHISPER THEM TO DADDY!

Daddy! The infantile endearment made him want to retch. It always had. "Do you have to call him Daddy when you're a grown woman?" he'd demanded of Meg.

Meg, looking hurt, slightly ill-used, had answered: "I don't have to, but I couldn't change now, even if I wanted to."

Daddy! A simper for ever on her lips. A name familiar to every one of the Red Man's spies. Spelt out on paper to harass and humiliate him . . .

At his shoulder Meg asked: "What have you got there?"

With a sleight of hand card and envelope were transferred to his pocket. "A tip for a horse in the 2.30 tomorrow. Some old tramp wheedled a bob out of me for it in The George at lunchtime."

She looked mildly surprised. "But you don't bet!"

"He wasn't to know that. He was a plausible old devil. Is that the evening paper you've got."

"It's just come. They've found her car."

It was headlined across the front page. "Police Find Murdered Girl's Car."

Ashley stared at the slightly fuzzed picture of it being loaded on to a police lorry against a backcloth of willows that stood behind the dewpond. After surveying, keeping a tag on six possible sites for ditching Monica's car, he'd opted for the forty-foot-deep pool, with shelving sides as the one presenting the least risk of observation. Under three miles from Keeper's Cottage, until the last quarter-mile he could approach it by a network of lanes and tracks over land that had been private property until tenants and owners had been dispossessed by the Water Board. With no workmen or technicians operating on Sunday, the whole area swept clean of house and farm-dwellers, provided he kept his eyes scanning forward, his ears pricked to reach cover in time, the chance of anyone seeing him was minimal. The last quarter-mile along a B road had spelled a risk, but there his luck had held. No one had passed him, and he hadn't seen a soul on his return journey to pick up his own car at Keeper's Cottage.

It was logical to assume that the police in their search for Monica's car had dredged every piece of deep water in the area, in due course worked round to the dewpond. So it became a flight of morbid fancy to allow himself to be tormented by the two cards in his pocket into a suspicion that someone had been lying hidden in the bracken, spying on his outward and return journeys . . . someone, for instance, who had a supply of filing cards and cheap buff envelopes, old scores to pay off against Ashley Jones. Or who had killed Monica, watched him bury her!

To be coerced into a nerve-storm of self-doubts was to play right into the feeble-witted jokester's hand. With a mental swipe he cleared his mind, smiled at Meg, enquired: "How is your father now? He sounds quiet enough."

"He's asleep."

"Then stop fretting." He handed her a drink. "Once he's really blown his top, he stays as quiet as a lamb for days."

"There is that," she said, with a grin of relief. "And Pip's gone off too. So, you're right, darling. Nothing in the world to worry about."

Richard Price was reading *The Wind in the Willows* to his six-and-a-half-year-old daughter, Jinny, who was sitting on the floor in a sugar-pink dressing-gown, fair hair tied in a bunch of curls on the crown of her head, one woolly slipper obscuring the headlines of the evening paper he'd brought home with him. She was fighting a two-pronged battle: to keep awake and to check her father's reading in case he skipped a paragraph.

She pounced. "You've missed out what Mole said."

"I'm sorry."

Sylvie called from the doorway: "Darling, you've had treble ration tonight. It's after seven. Come on, now."

As a matter of principle Jinny protested, gripped her father's leg with her stalk-like arms, but in the end she capitulated, and he was left with the scent of soap in his nostrils, the headline in the newspaper on the carpet.

He wadded it tight, dumped it in the waste-paper basket, a gesture he acknowledged to be both cowardly and futile. After supper Sylvie would ask him for it. Anyway, the news would be repeated in the morning paper. He retrieved it, smoothed it out, put it on the table.

When she came back into the room, though her glance skimmed it, she said with no visible perturbation: "I saw the placard when I fetched Jinny from school, so I bought one." She came forward, placed an arm round his shoulder, mused: "You wouldn't think any car could last that long, would you? But it is the same one she used to run around in. Whoever murdered her, drove it into that pond, counted on it never coming to light. Finding it should help them, shouldn't it?"

"Who, the police? I suppose so."

They stayed enclosed in silence for almost a minute, and then she moved away to set the place mats on the table in the dining alcove. Half-way through she whirled round to face him.

"Ricky, do you know what I've been wishing all day?"

"No, tell me."

She came back to his side, and with a sudden breaking of composure that shook him badly, buried her head against his chest, so that he had to listen hard to hear what she said.

". . . that those boys had never found her. That there'd been no drought and the reservoir had stayed full of water, so that she'd just melted away . . . there'd been nothing to find . . . ever."

Contrite, she lifted her head. "Aren't you ashamed of me, actually wanting to obstruct the course of justice . . . wanting whoever murdered her to go free?"

"Ashamed of you?" he queried lovingly. "How could that ever be! All I want is to be able to keep my promise to make you happy."

She wasn't a woman who cried easily either from joy or sorrow, but now she could feel the weight of unshed tears pressing on her eyeballs. "I am happy. I couldn't be anything else with you . . ." She gave a shaky, apologetic sigh. "It's only that I long for it to be over, finished . . . Never to have to read Monica's name in print again." She laughed scorn upon herself. "I ought to have more sense, but every time I hear the doorbell, I start shivering in case it's the police."

He said, helplessness making him weak: "Darling, I'd give anything to stop you worrying. . . . Please, try not to. There's no need."

She moved back to the table, put down the last place mat, said quietly: "This morning, before you were awake, I suddenly had second thoughts, got to wondering if we'd handled it right. Wouldn't it have been easier on us, in the long run, if you'd gone to the police, told them that you'd been her husband? What do you think?"

His reaction was an explosively curt negative: "No." When she said nothing, he added in a serious, persuasive tone: "Why embroil ourselves? I'm under no legal compulsion. It would probably mean we'd find ourselves in the newspapers . . . 'all about us' so to speak. Reporters badger police officers in a murder case, so that to fight them off, they throw them any odd, sometimes quite irrelevant, scrap of news that will get into print, show the public they're not letting the grass grow under their feet. We'd be good for half a column!"

She gave him a look that was haunted by secret images common to both of them, said quietly: "It was a mad idea, forget it." She forced a smile. "Maybe there'll be some beautiful clue in the car that will send the police marching up to the door of whoever murdered her. Do you think there's a chance?"

"I don't know. Let's hope so."

Chapter 8

One of the heaviest crosses Frederick Gasson was called on to bear was that for twenty-four hours a day he was on public view, with no niche of privacy, no shelter behind which he might retire, perform some trivial act that would remain unknown to anyone but himself. Though he admitted in advance it was futile, every so often he was driven to rebellion.

On Wednesday morning, he ordered Hexham to fetch the box containing Goodsell's old service revolver, ammunition from the back of the sideboard in the dining-room. He dawdled infernally long over a simple errand, and when he returned, Frederick saw why. Meg had ambushed him. It was she who was carrying the flat wooden box, pawing at the heavy knotted cord, face alight with curiosity.

"It weighs a ton. Daddy, what on earth's in it? Shall I open it for you?"

"I don't want it opened. Put it on the bed."

"But what's in it?" she insisted.

"Papers," he snapped. "Give it to me."

"Papers and what else? Gold sovereigns!" Reluctantly, after dusting it off, she put it within his reach. "Those knots are much too tight to undo. Shall I fetch some scissors?"

"No, leave it." Desperately he tried a foolproof distraction. "How's Pip this morning?"

"Better. He ate his breakfast, thank goodness. Aren't you going to let me see what's in that old box?"

"No. So you can stop asking."

When she'd gone, still throwing offended and slightly suspicious glances backwards over her shoulder, he ordered Hexham to stow it in the top drawer of his bedside cabinet. Even that wasn't a simple operation because it was already half full with his current box of cigars, handkerchiefs and an ample supply of the humiliating bibs that were tied round his neck before meals.

When it was safely out of sight, he thought bitterly, to what end? What good was a gun to him, tied up in a box, not even loaded, out of reach without a struggle that would bring him to the point of collapse? To be effective it had to be put in his hand, and then, maybe with Ashley positioned two feet away, he might summon up the strength to pull the trigger. Would they put a paralysed man in gaol for life? And if they did, would it be worth it? On balance, he was inclined to say yes.

When Hexham came back from washing the dust off his hands, he ordered: "Get me the Bank. I want to speak to that fool of a manager." That was another of his blisters of resentment: his fingers weren't reliable on a telephone dial.

The number obtained, Mr Tyson on the other end, Hexham went out, closed the door behind him. That was the rule when Mr Gasson was telephoning.

He found Meg in the kitchen strapping Pip into his pram. The last buckle secure, she turned on him. "Mr Hexham, about the weekend. Honestly, it's not worth all this fuss you've made about going, if you don't start your break till Saturday. Won't you, to please me, leave after you've given my father his lunch on Friday? It's Elsie's day here, and I know if I ask her she'll stay until my husband gets home."

"No," he said, made forceful to the point of rudeness by his dismay at the re-opening of an argument he'd believed closed. With an effort he tempered his voice. "My arrangements are made, Mrs Jones. My mother does not expect me until Saturday afternoon."

Frustrated, she put Pip into the patch of shade by the back door. Coming back her foot brushed against a basket of laundry. As she bent to tuck in an overhanging shirt sleeve, the frown she'd worn was swept away, and when she stood up, he sensed that she hardly remembered he was there.

With his deep involvement of heart that contained neither hope nor ambition, but was a simple state of existence, the gesture, its aftermath, were as plain as if he'd experienced them himself. She'd caressed a scrap of man-made fibre because Ashley had worn it, would soon be wearing it again. Without bitterness he accepted the outlandish nature of his love, the payment it exacted in that he was no longer one person but two, subjected to the strains of Meg's life as well as his own. In spirit he lived with her for twenty-four hours a day.

She blinked, returned briskly to the task of making him see sense. "Mr Hexham, I don't want to appear nosy, but you seem so . . . well . . . reluctant to visit your mother, don't you enjoy seeing her? And if you don't, why not spend your free-time somewhere else?"

He wondered how she would react if he answered: Can you enjoy visiting a woman whose every breath comes out of a great lung of hate? If he died, his mother, left with no hate to sustain her, would die too.

"It's rather that we no longer have much in common. We've grown apart. It's not unusual in parents and adult children!"

"I suppose so," she admitted half-heartedly, as though not wanting to believe what she conceded. "Is your father alive?"

"No." As neatly decapitated by the smashed windscreen of the car his son had been driving as if he had put his head on the block of a guillotine.

"No brothers and sisters?"

"No." Though the report from the hospital had been D.O.A., there'd been a tiny pulse of life in his sister when the ambulance men lifted her out of the gutter into which she'd been thrown by the head-on collision. Watching the driver of the car he'd hit trying to drag the mangled body of his wife clear of the wreckage in which she was trapped, hearing the lorry driver he'd overtaken screaming in the manic hysteria of shock: "You bloody murderer! Hanging's too good for your sort," he'd clung, for the sake of sanity, to the belief that his parents' only other child would live. But his prayer had gone unanswered.

Meg touched his hand. "Mr Hexham, forgive me. I should know by now that you dislike talking about yourself. I'm sorry. I didn't mean to upset you." Her stance was coltish, her smile engagingly ingenuous. "My husband is always telling me I've no tact, and how right he is!"

"Please," he begged, embarrassed at finding his voice unsteady, "there's no need . . ." Before he could get it under control, the air was riven by Mr Gasson's bell.

At eleven, when he'd fed his patient a mid-morning drink, settled him for a pre-lunch nap, he went to the greenhouse. Alone, picking a trug of ripe tomatoes for Meg, he strove to rationalise—and reason away—his obsession of fear. Start by reliving that winter afternoon now two and a half years old.

He had been walking back to his patient via the outskirts of Helton, the ice left by the frost of the night before still

glazing the pavements, when he was jerked out of his per-
petual state of self-absorption by the piercing screams of a
child. He'd swung about, seen a boy of ten or so lying on
the road under a bicycle he'd been tumbled off by a car
that had taken the corner too sharply.

The paralysis of reincarnated horror that any street accident induced, rendered him incapable of movement as
he watched a woman beside the driver of the car clawing
at his arm, yelling at him to stop. He did so, level with him.
The girl tumbled out, went running awkwardly on high heels
till she reached the child, dragged him free of the crumpled
wheels. By then memory was losing its crippling hold, his
limbs were unfrozen, and he was able to hasten after her to
an accompaniment of upflung doors and windows, through
which women shouted wanting to know what had happened.

The two of them had stood the boy on his feet, inspected
a graze along one cheekbone, shallow but messy cuts on
both knees. They'd taken him into the nearest open door,
and he'd stayed to bind up his knees, sponge his face clear
of tears and blood.

"Is he all right?" the girl from the car had demanded
anxiously. "You don't think we should call an ambulance?"

When he'd reassured her, she'd taken an envelope out of
her handbag, written on it, handed it to the boy. "That's
my name, Monica Price, and where I live. You take the bike
along to be mended, ask the man how much it will be,
then come and collect the money from me." She'd turned
up his chin with her thumb. "And next time ride a bit closer
to the curb."

Leaving the boy in charge of the housewife who promised
to see him home to the next street, they'd walked out together. When they'd come level with the car, she'd
thanked him, said goodbye, then as she got into her seat,

he'd overheard her explode into a paean of rage. "You callous devil. That kid might have been seriously hurt. You could at least have had the common decency to find out. One of these days you're going to kill someone. Not that you'd care!"

Before he'd walked on, he'd taken a curious glance at the face of the driver, who was sitting placidly smoking, utterly divorced from the scene of violence and alarm that had erupted about him. On it he recognised instantly that inborn inability to respond to a cry of pain that marks the born psychopath: amoral, anti-social, existing in his own hermetically sealed sphere, all creatures without utterly worthless, expendable at whim.

A lightning diagnosis at which mental specialists would have jeered? Indubitably, but three years as a probationary nurse in a hospital for the mentally sick had left him with a measure of diagnostic skill.

He'd never seen the driver again, known his name, until his first evening at Laburnum Lodge when Mrs Jones had said: "Mr Hexham, I would like you to meet my husband."

And the girl who'd jumped out of the car, mopped up the boy's tears with her scarf, had been murdered, shoved into a grave soon to be drowned under a million tons of water. But the waters to someone's horror had receded, exposed the brutal fact of murder.

One card at the office on Monday; one at home on Tuesday. On Wednesday morning Ashley had been braced for a third heckling taunt to drop through the letter-box at Laburnum Lodge or be laid uppermost on Mrs Wisley's pyramid of post. When it didn't appear in either place, a question mark remained over the afternoon delivery, with the possibility that it would reach the Red Man, spark off a repeat performance of yesterday's little scene.

Maybe the clever know-all had run out of permutations on Keep! His resentment was as furious as if someone had daubed a picture he had painted. After Monica's first telephone call, ordering him to meet her, he'd set about searching for the perfect site, somewhere far beyond the range of the Red Man's spies. And he'd found it. Keeper's Cottage. As he'd anticipated Monica's reaction had been a flat no. "We're only going to talk for ten minutes. What do you take me for, a girl guide out to win a wood-trekking badge? Pick somewhere else."

But he'd stubbornly refused. In the end, because it amused her to think he was so scared he wouldn't meet her unless there was no one visible for miles, she'd agreed.

And when she'd doled out his fourteen days' grace, and he'd said: "Right, same time and place?" she hadn't cared about anything but getting her greedy hands on the money. "Okay, here, if you want. Just so long as you're not scheming to double-cross me! For instance, don't try to plant a witness behind a tree or a heap of stones."

Which was probably why she'd taken the precaution of arriving early to beat over the ground. But had she missed one? Had he? No, he reassured himself, he had not. He was as secure from suspicion as he'd ever been. He would not be rattled by a kids' sneaky game played by one of the Red Man's spies, any more than he'd allowed himself to be made jittery by the sight of Sergeant Trent posted outside the entrance as he drove into Gasson's that morning. Though he'd been at pains to wave a friendly hello, Sergeant Trent, normally an affable man given to kow-towing to his superiors when an opportunity arose, had not responded but hung about to watch him park the car, before he'd plodded on. So what? Even at 9 A.M. the temperature had been soaring, the pavement unkind to the feet that had to pound a beat for a living. Or maybe Sergeant Trent had merely had a row with his wife over breakfast!

As he opened the door of the salesroom to usher out Mrs Crankshaw who had paid her fourth visit to inspect a car she had no money to buy, he saw Libby having her Aston Martin filled at the pumps. Her head was thrown back and she was laughing at some joke the attendant had made, showing off her flaming hair, low-cut lemon shift. As he turned away he reflected idly that if he'd ever been in a position to exercise a free choice over a wife, Libby came pretty near to fitting the bill.

On his way back to his office he collected the carbons of last month's orders from Mrs Wisley. She parted with them grudgingly, in a manner which suggested they were no business of his.

But today they were. Customers' names and addresses were written in block capitals. He wanted to compare Tony's order sheets with the two cards in his pocket. He was leafing through them when Vanessa, taking any opportunity to edge her person into his view, opened his door to usher Libby in.

His "hello" contained a note of genuine surprise. He couldn't remember her ever calling on him at the office.

She sat down across the desk, spoke in her favourite tone of voice that contained an innuendo of secret knowingness. "Since I was here, I just looked in to make sure Saturday's okay for you and Meg."

"All set." In his head Ashley counted the days between him and his dead-line, suppressed a leap of desperation. "How many have you got coming?"

"Seventy-five or so." She bent across the desk to take a light for her cigarette so letting him see she wasn't wearing a bra. She leaned back to exhale, cloud the air between them with a wreath of smoke. "Also, I was nosy enough to wonder how you'd been faring with the police . . . about Monica."

So that was why Libby was sitting where she was! He shrugged his shoulders. "We've come to a dead end. I've told them all I can, which is precious little. Monica and I were through by then."

"Only just," she suggested softly. "Or that was how it looked to me in a ringside seat."

"But through," he insisted.

The eyes that were a pure green in the bright light of the gold-fish bowl considered him before she teased: "Have it your way; I admit it sounds better. Superintendent Ross and one of his little men paid us a visit . . . Sunday, I think it was. Not that we could help. Ian never knew her, and as for me, I couldn't tell them anything . . . Well, could I, darling?"

He smiled tolerantly to imply he had no idea what she was talking about.

"For instance," she went on, her eyes slanted to keep a watch on his face, "this money she wanted to borrow to buy that dreadful, tatty gift shop in the High Street, she tried to tap you, didn't she?"

"Me!" The shock of dismay didn't matter. It could be taken for genuine astonishment. "What gave you that extraordinary idea?"

"Monica. We ran into one another one evening in the Pelican. I was waiting for Tony, and she was alone at the bar, a bit tight. She knew Dad was a bank manager, and though we'd never been introduced, she told me about the shop, angled to find out what hope she'd got of raising a loan from him. With her security, or lack of it, I could hardly be optimistic, could I? I asked her why she didn't shop around for a private loan among her friends. She didn't react, not until you and Tony came in, with Meg behind you, all sheepy and embarrassed because she was scared her father would get to hear about her drinking in pubs. Monica gave you a long, long look, and quite suddenly she cheered up."

"Look!" he exclaimed. "You've the gall to tell me you remember a look, all that time ago!"

"There are some looks you never forget. When someone's horse romps home first; or he's let off a hook on which he's been dangling for years. For instance, I remember your look the night Tony gave that house-warming party. Like a cat who's burgled the larder, lapped up all the cream, and however much anyone raves, there's damn-all they can do to take it away from him. Meg promised to marry you that night, didn't she?"

"Somewhere around then, I suppose."

"*That night*. On your way home from Tony's. Meg phoned me next morning, for comfort and support. She'd just broken the news to her father!"

"Actually, I asked her to marry me three times."

"But the night of Tony's party was when she said yes." She stood up abruptly to intimate that a denial was pointless.

In the second's delay before he rose, glancing upwards, he caught a new expression on her face, neither jibing nor lit from behind by secret amusement, but one of uncharacteristic gravity that made it almost a stranger's. A moment later when she flipped her hand at him, it had vanished. "Bye. Give Meg my love. See you on Saturday."

When he was alone he went back to examining the block-lettered names and addresses of Tony's customers. But echoes of phrases, innuendoes she'd left behind disrupted his concentration. A look, he thought with searing resentment, that anyone should have hoarded up a word, a gesture incriminating him years after it should have been obliterated past resurrection! And Libby claiming to know positively that Monica, searching for a gold mine, had picked him.

A look! By now his silent exclamation had turned to derision. A look wasn't evidence, and the police already knew that Monica was trying to raise money. But not from whom. And they never would.

Painstakingly he combed through the orders, comparing the block letters with the cards. In a few he detected a similarity; in others none. Tony could have been responsible for the two messages in gibberish tucked in his wallet. Equally, so could any other member of the Red Man's band of spies.

There was no cheap buff envelope on the hall table where Meg normally left the few letters—mostly bills—that came to him at the house. Neither was one visible in the cautious sweep he made from the doorway of the horizontal surfaces of the Red Man's bedroom. The wire frame supporting the newspaper he was reading shielded the Red Man's face until he was inside the room. He stepped softly, aiming to materialise suddenly, catch his enemy by surprise, which was a form of entrance that set off an explosion of rage.

But the surprise was his. The Red Man had fallen down on his evening vigil. He was asleep, disgustingly so, mouth agape, a trickle of slimy spittle on his chin. Wax finger and thumb of his right hand had gone slack about the butt of a cigar tipped into the huge onyx ash-tray resting on the quilt. The left-hand thumb was on the flex of his bell as if sleep had overtaken him before he could push the button that resulted in ear-shattering buzz-blasts sounding off in Hexham's room and the hall.

With catlike stealth Ashley walked to the foot of the bed, a vantage point from which he could survey the whole room. The door into the bathroom was, for once, tight closed. Was there an eye or an ear at the keyhole? Taking no chances he behaved as if he were under surveillance, touching nothing, letting his swivelling eyes do all the work. He weighed the difference between this time and the hours from midnight on Saturday till dawn on Sunday. Three. It would not be Hexham who'd be guarding the Red Man, but Meg, who'd insist on moving downstairs. The electric fan would not be purring. There'd be darkness instead of light.

Deliberately he emptied his mind, carrying out a mental sweeping operation that banished all the petty bedevilments of the last eight days, leaving it clean, weightless. And then, confirming his faith in himself, inspiration surfaced, transcribed itself on the spotless planes he'd prepared for it. So absurdly simple that he'd gasped that it hadn't done so months ago. Obvious, so hand-tooled for the seeming self-destruction of the Red Man that he was left shaking his head at the delayed functioning of his wits.

With care not to disturb the sleeping heap in the bed, he placed the day's reports by the side of the bell-push, made a noiseless exit.

Meg, coming downstairs, opened her lips to cry a welcome. He put a finger to his mouth to order her to silence, then with elaborate caution tip-toed towards the sitting-room.

"He's asleep," he said when she caught up with him. "It seemed a pity to wake him."

She drew back from kissing him. "I'm glad. It's been one of his black days. He's been so depressed that neither Hexham nor I could get a smile out of him. He wasn't even interested in Pip. Maybe he'll feel better when he wakes up."

She leaned forward to look into his face, exclaimed with delight: "Darling, you look on top of the world. Has something nice happened? Made a big sale?"

He laughed. "Nothing. I just feel good."

"You look it." She stood close to his shoulder as he poured her sherry, made shy and gauche by the intensity of her emotion. "I'm glad, darling. I mind terribly that often you're not happy, that you can't be. But it's no good brooding on it, talking endlessly about it, is it? We can't change anything."

"I don't want you to change anything, my love. We're all right."

"We are, aren't we?" she said gratefully. She sipped, put her glass down suddenly. "I nearly forgot. Tony rang. He said it was such an age since he'd seen us together, and it is, weeks, could he look in after supper. He'll be here about eight."

Chapter 9

Richard Price saw the police car the instant he stepped out of the taxi. Parked alongside the main entrance, with no police insignia, it could have been any car, with any two men sitting in front. Only a sixth sense he'd developed in the last week flashed a warning that they were detectives who had spent effort and ingenuity in tracking him down and were now waiting, with all the stolid patience of those who are accustomed to wait, for him to talk.

As *he'd* waited for them, praying that they'd never arrive, that before they'd ploughed through dreary, time-wasting records of births, deaths, divorces, the telephone directories of an unknown number of towns that would inevitably bring them to his door, they'd have arrested for murder some man of whom he'd never heard, lost all interest in Richard Edward Price. It had been a gamble, with the odds against him. He'd lost. Now for the next one.

As he put his key into the lock he didn't deny his fear, but it was fear reduced to manageable proportions by his relief that a full hour remained before Sylvie was due home. At half-past three she'd left the flat with Jinny to drive to a children's party ten miles away. That was why he'd not taken the car that morning. "Expect me around seven," she'd said. "I always stay on to give Sally a hand with clearing up, and then she usually insists on my having a drink. But not later than seven."

Suddenly a jet of fear spurted, dousing relief. How long had they been waiting? Had they caught Sylvie, catechised her before she left. No. If they had she'd have telephoned him at the office.

Inside the living-room he stood in frozen stillness, waiting for the doorbell to announce curtain-up on his ordeal by question. He'd spent eight nights rehearsing his part until he believed he was word perfect, with all the right gestures, facial expressions on tap. He'd even allowed himself the small vanity of including his person—grave, distinguished, vaguely academic, utterly responsible—among his assets. Coupled with the high esteem in which he was held by his employers, it made palpable nonsense of the rough and tumble of a police interrogation about a murder.

When the doorbell did ring he went straight into his part, looking with polite puzzlement at the two men waiting in the hallway. "Yes?"

The senior officer went perfunctorily through the routine of flipping an identity card. "Mr Richard Price? We're County Police. I'm Detective Superintendent Ross, and this is Detective Sergeant Hallam. I wonder if we might have a word with you?"

Except that in anticipation their faces had been blanks, the scene was so precisely as he'd imagined it, that he experienced a sense of *déjà vu*. "Of course, come in. This way."

Ross took the chair in which Sylvie usually sat, Hallam an occasional one by the window. He sat in his own, directing a questioning but pacific glance at Ross, aware that his opening words must be captious, if not frankly accusing.

"Mr Price, I don't have to waste time explaining why we are here. I am in charge of the investigation into the murder of your divorced wife, Monica Price, whose body was found eight days ago in the Dene Valley Reservoir. The case has received wide publicity in the national press, on radio and television. You can't have remained unaware that we were appealing for you to contact us to help in our enquiries. I'd like to know why you failed to do this."

He gave his answer with the firm confidence of one who had nothing to fear. "Because to me Monica has literally been dead for six years. There was nothing I could tell you that could have had the least bearing on her murder. If I'd been able to assist you in the smallest way, I would, of course, have contacted you. As I couldn't, I decided it would be a waste of my time and yours to do so."

Pointedly Ross said nothing, leaving his expression of outright disbelief and flat condemnation to answer for him. "When did you last see her?"

"Six years ago, in the Law Courts on the day of the divorce. I never saw her again, had the remotest idea where she was living."

Ross demanded on much the same brusque note of authority that Richard had anticipated in a police interrogation: "How long have you lived in this flat, Mr Price?"

"Five years next month."

"You moved in a year after your divorce. Is that when you entered the employment of the plastics firm for whom you now work?"

"Yes."

"Where you are now the deputy manager?"

"Yes."

"I'd like to know about your marriage, Mr Price."

He set his mouth into a line of grave repugnance. "It was a disaster. From the beginning to the end. We were completely incompatible."

"Your wife divorced you, naming as co-respondent a woman called Sylvia Ann Markham, née Harris, correct?"

"Yes."

"Have you any children, Mr Price?"

"One, a daughter." He met full on the hard eyes, over one of which the lid dipped sharply, from which he could expect no mercy, waited with a tightening of nerves for Ross to ask: "How old?" but the question didn't come. Which meant they knew already, either from looking up the registration of Jinny's birth, or from asking round the flats. He'd schooled himself to accept that if they did arrive it would be armed with a fat dossier filled with every detail about him on which they'd been able to lay their hands. Even so, he had to work hard to appear unmoved by the rat-tat of questions, the answers recorded in Sergeant Hallam's notebook.

"Mr Price, did you pay your wife alimony?"

"No. She preferred a lump sum, a complete severance. She received from me fifteen hundred pounds, and I paid the rent of the flat until the end of the lease, which had a year to run. She also took the car."

Ross extracted a paper from his pocket, consulted it, while Sergeant Hallam, with a disinterested expression stared at Sylvie's collection of porcelain birds.

Ross's head jerked up from the paper in his hands. "Why did Sylvia Markham not obtain a divorce from her husband, James Markham?"

He'd prepared his answer, but somehow it wouldn't slide quickly off his tongue. Waiting for it, Ross added a footnote: "Mr Price, I'd like to emphasise that it is of no concern to the police whether you and Sylvia Price as she now is by right of deed poll have gone through a marriage ceremony."

"Then why do you ask?"

"Because if your former wife was aware that you weren't legally married to the woman who is known as your wife she might conceivably have been blackmailing you. Have you any prospect of marrying?"

"Not in her husband's lifetime. There is a religious bar. He is a Roman Catholic."

"Did your divorced wife ever try to exploit the unhappy situation in which you were placed, threaten to tell your neighbours, employer, the parents of your daughter's school-friends if you did not make it worth her while to keep quiet?"

"She wasn't in a position to. She didn't know where I lived. I've told you already that there has been no communication between us since the divorce."

"How long had you known Sylvia Markham before your wife divorced you?"

"Two years."

"Your former wife made no objection to the divorce?"

"No. For both of us the marriage was completely dead. For some time we hadn't been living together. Provided her terms were met, which was literally to take every penny I then possessed, she welcomed the divorce."

Ross allowed his steely glance to swing slowly round the room. "You have a very pleasant home, Mr Price. Haven't you done rather well for yourself . . . attained a higher income bracket than your former wife might have anticipated at the time of your divorce?"

"I've been fortunate in that I joined a new and expanding company. Also since the divorce, Sylvie . . . my wife . . . inherited a legacy from her mother. She has a private income of her own."

"Mr Price, I must ask you again, are you prepared to state categorically that your divorced wife, Monica Price, never made any attempt to blackmail you?"

"Yes."

"She never sought to make contact with you?"

"I have already answered that question. The answer is still no."

"Thank you. Now, if you don't mind, I'd like to go back to the last weekend in May two years ago. We believe that Monica Price was murdered on May thirtieth, or in the early hours of May thirty-first. How did you spend that day?"

"Superintendent! I'm sorry, I have absolutely no idea."

"Let's approach it from a different angle. What do you normally do on a fine Sunday in late spring. That particular Sunday was mild and dry, no rain until late evening."

"I would probably have stayed around the flat in the morning, maybe taken Jinny down to the beach while my wife finished off dinner. If it was a particularly pleasant day we might have gone for a drive in the afternoon, but whether we did or not . . ." he shrugged helplessly.

"Then, let me ask this question, Mr Price. Can you recall varying your routine on any May Sunday two years ago?"

"No." A wink of alarm warned him that he'd come to the end of all the answers he'd rehearsed. From now on he must ad lib.

Ross who'd spent the moment staring into space above his head, came to life abruptly. "Mr Price, do you know Helton?"

"No."

"Keeper's Cottage in Dene Valley that was flooded when they built a new reservoir?"

"I have never been to Helton, or to Dene Valley."

With a backward sweep of his arm Ross held out his hand to Hallam, snapped his fingers in command. On cue, Hallam rose, delivered a small piece of paper encased in cellophane. Ross held it out. "Take it, Mr Price. Not very legible, I fear, but I think you can make it out."

Richard gazed until his sight blurred, trying to keep his ballooning panic under control.

Ross said conversationally: "As you see, it is a sketch-map of the route between Brighton and Dene Valley Reservoir. The site of Keeper's Cottage is marked, though the map is a little smudged in that corner. In the circumstances that's to be expected."

In what circumstances? It was the map Monica had sent him. Where he'd lost it was more important than answering Ross's question. Except that he couldn't have lost it: along with the letters she'd addressed to him at the office he had burnt it, flushed the ashes down the sink. So why was his flesh cold, his brain numb? Ross wasn't a magician who could change ash back into paper. "Yes, that's what it appears to be."

"Have you seen it before?"

"No." He made his voice excessively casual. "Am I allowed to ask where you found it?"

"In the inner compartment of a notecase in Monica Price's handbag, in her car. It was protected by mica, otherwise, immersed in water, it wouldn't have remained as legible as it is."

Some crevice in his brain had been busy solving the riddle for him. Monica had scribbled the route out for him, then recopied it, kept the original. Absently he was beginning to turn it over, when Ross reached out, snatched it out of his hand, gave it back into Hallam's keeping, leaving Richard with an imprecise impression of writing on the reverse side . . . which Ross obviously had not wished him to examine.

"Mr Price, have you ever travelled from Brighton to Dene Valley?"

"Never."

"Do you know if your former wife had friends in Brighton whom she might have invited to visit her?"

He opened his mouth and found that his well of self-control had run dry. "My God! how many more times do I have to spell it out for you. I've not the remotest idea where Monica's friends lived . . . if she had any."

The dipping lid of Ross's right eye lifted itself as he demanded: "By what name did your former wife call you?"

The shock of losing control over his temper, the seemingly irrelevant question thrown at him, had a mildly stupefying effect on Richard. "Would you mind repeating that?"

"By what name were you known to your former wife?"

"Richard."

"Never by a diminutive: Ricky or Dick?"

"Never."

"Immediately before she was murdered she was in communication with two people whose initials were respectively: D.D. and H.R.H. Can you put names to them, Mr Price?"

"No, I can't," he said flatly. "I don't know anyone to whom they might apply."

"You're positive?"

"Quite positive."

They went soon afterwards, but taking their time over their exit, dawdling, it seemed to his tortured nerves, in case another question should occur to them. It was five minutes to seven when their car drove out of the fore-court. Three minutes later when Sylvie came in. But at least the gap, tiny as it was, had been there to protect her.

One of Tony's more irritating affectations was the act he put on of being Meg's devoted slave. Tonight, for instance, he had kissed her hand, declared she looked ravishing—in a floral house dress in which she'd bathed Pip, hair in lank rat-tails—and made a full-scale production out of giving her a huge, gaudily beribboned box of chocolates, the kind half-filled with paper shavings. Thanking him, she'd pecked his cheek with a kiss; whereupon Tony had pretended to swoon with delight.

At least, until now, Ashley had always assumed it was an act. But as the three of them lounged by the French window to catch any stray wafts of breeze, he asked himself whether Tony, in that appallingly vulgar flat, had the overwhelming conceit to indulge in a fantasy of seeing himself as the young master of Laburnum Lodge, the husband of the Red Man's heiress. If so, it was pitiful.

Then, from far away he was alerted by a buzz of doubt. Surely, even Tony, would require some platform of firm expectation on which to erect such a preposterous pyramid of hope? So what had he used for bricks? Defamation of her husband's character was a paper sword where Meg was concerned. One criticising word and she'd spring like an avenging Amazon to his defence. The serious nature of the charges against him Tony had somehow contrived to lay before the police? He shouted that one down. Tony knew nothing. He was as powerless to scare him as the silly, hectoring bleep coming from the cards lying in his wallet.

Meg exclaimed happily: "Ashley's on top of the world tonight. Just look at him! I wish he'd let me into the secret. I suspect he's plotting some heavenly surprise. He's marvellous at surprises."

"Euphoria!" Tony pronounced waggishly. "Careful, old man, it's a sure-fire way to tempt fate. That's when she sneaks up on you, stabs you in the back."

"Tony!" Meg protested.

"Only my little joke, darling." He squeezed her hand in a plea for forgiveness as he examined Ashley. "Now you mention it, he does look unusually chipper. Come on, Ashley, share the good news."

"None from me. I'm all agog for you to entertain us with the latest crime bulletin. What have your little flock of tame birds been whispering in your ear lately? Isn't that what you came to tell us?"

"Oh, Ashley," Meg wailed, "not the murder, not tonight. It's such a lovely evening, I don't want it spoilt."

"You're right, my love, as you invariably are," Tony said fulsomely.

Ashley smiled winningly at them both. "But Tony claims he has private sources of information. If that is so, it's mean of him to hold out on his friends. Errol Simpson, roosting outside Ross's door, keeps him up to date. That's so, isn't it, Tony?"

Tony said priggishly: "I may have privileged contacts, and I'm not denying there have been developments, but I am not at liberty . . ."

"To divulge confidential information," Ashley finished for him. "But I'm beginning to wonder if you have any, or whether it isn't just a tale you're spinning."

Tony bristled with self-importance. "The police have a strong suspect."

"Good," Meg said. "What a relief! That means it will soon be over."

"How can you be positive they've got a suspect?" Ashley asked.

"If you know something about police methods, and I flatter myself I do, you become extraordinarily sensitive to atmosphere. When, after following a dozen false trails, they get their noses on the right scent, you can actually feel it. In this case, someone dropped in, handed in a piece of vital information. And there they are, all set for the kill."

"Who dropped by?"

Tony pursed his fat little mouth self-righteously, as Meg said firmly: "Ashley, that's enough. I don't want to know. Pour us another drink."

Temporarily Ashley gave up. "We seem to be running short of soda. I'll go and recharge the siphon."

Some unspecified while later he found himself standing in the hall, with no recollection of how he came to be there. For a long moment panic held him in a missed heart-beat of time before a wild spasm of rage ripped through him. God, not again!

It was the sight of Sam Goodsell emerging backwards through the Red Man's door that pulled him to rights, sent him running for reassurance behind a smokescreen of pretence that it hadn't happened. Old Sam making off after his Wednesday evening cribbage session, not actually tight, but light-headed and heavy-footed with whisky, scented with the smoke of rich cigars.

"Hello, Sam, on your way home?"

Awkwardly, in slow motion, as if reluctant to confirm that Ashley was there, the old man turned his grizzled head, slack mouth agape, while clutching defensively a box wedged between arm and ribs.

Suspecting he was about to drop it, Ashley stepped forward. "That looks heavy, Sam. Want me to give you a hand? What have you got in it?"

"No, thank you, sir. No thanks. It's all right. I can manage. It's not heavy. Don't you bother, sir. . . ."

A gabble of refusals that provided somewhat frenzied background music to Sam's scuttling retreat through the front door, leaving Ashley curious as to what was in the box. Something Sam had brought to show the Red Man? Something the Red Man had given him? Then why the gibbering dismay, guilty reaction at being caught with it, as if he'd stolen it?

Impatiently he threw the incident out of his head. It didn't matter a damn. What did was that, once again, the cogs of his memory had failed to knit.

He lifted the siphon on the hall table. Full. Which meant he had walked from the living-room all the way to the kitchen, opened the door of the wine cupboard, recharged the siphon, returned to the hall . . . minutes that were sealed in impenetrable darkness.

Panic such as he'd never experienced leaped alive in him. If he'd forgotten . . . But he hadn't. He knew precisely how the Red Man was going to die.

Tony called from behind: "There you are! Thought you were lost. Sorry, but as far as I'm concerned you've had a wasted journey. Time I made for my beddy-byes."

Meg chided: "What on earth happened to you? You've been an age."

"Sorry, I was seeing Sam out. He's just left."

Tony made a ceremony out of kissing Meg's hand; she a semblance of protest while loving every moment of it.

"Bye, Tony," she said, blushing furiously. "See you at Libby's on Saturday."

Over Meg's head Tony's glance flicked impudently, slyly into Ashley's. "Then we can expect the pleasure of your company?"

"Unless Sister Melton drops dead and we're left without a sitter."

"Ashley!" Meg turned on him. "Don't say such things, even as a joke. Of course we'll be there."

As she held the door wide for him, Tony said into her ear: "It's too late to bother your father again. Give him a message from me, will you? Say that if I have any definite news for him, I'll telephone him about noon tomorrow."

When she'd closed the door, Meg went straight into her

father's room to deliver the message, then asked: "What news are you expecting from Tony?"

"Business."

She grinned down at him tolerantly. "What a one you are for secrets! You always were. I remember when I was little you used to make a huge mystery out of the silliest things. Then I loved it. Now, I don't. I prefer to know what's going on."

"You're a woman. All women always want to know everything, even what's not good for them."

"That's your story," she said, kissing him. "I hope you have a good night. I'll call Hexham for you."

And when they'd all left him, and the house was silent about and over him, he looked back over the evening's work with a small measure of satisfaction. The pistol, which Sam had loaded, was in the top drawer of his bedside cabinet, under the cover of a pile of handkerchiefs. To aim and fire it would call for exertion of which he was not always capable. He'd have to trust to luck that he'd find that reserve of strength if he needed it. If . . . if . . . the infuriating badgering of that word set his teeth grinding.

What Tony West told him, what Sam retailed of what he'd picked up from Sergeant Trent; Mrs Wisley's reports, the remarks Tom Norris let drop. And every syllable of it second-hand! It occurred to him that maybe what he ought to do was to call Ross, order him to Laburnum Lodge.

But he'd wait, at least until Tony telephoned in the morning. In the last resort there was always the pistol. He'd been sorry at having to involve Sam, but Sam was a good liar. He'd sworn him to secrecy, so that if anyone, afterwards, put any awkward questions to him, he could be relied upon to play the innocent. Sam was a wily old bird; he wouldn't be likely to let anyone catch him with the box and spare ammunition before he disposed of it.

Chapter 10

During the early hours of Thursday morning, Mrs Wisley's personal nemesis struck. At 8 A.M. her husband, on her whispered instructions, telephoned Tom Norris. Not Mr Jones? He queried. But even with the room swimming around her, shreds of light through the drawn curtains piercing her eye-balls with daggers, nausea near uncontainable, she'd managed to shake her head.

Face aglow, thanking heaven she was wearing the salmon tricel dress she'd bought on Saturday afternoon, that stopped short five inches above her knees, Vanessa skimmed down the showroom to greet Mr Jones the moment he appeared.

"Mrs Wisley's got another of her migraines. Her husband phoned Mr Norris, and after I'd been waiting ages he let me in with his key." She paused for him to get her point: for once, she'd been on time. She made a totally unnecessary adjustment to the wisp of material over her shoulder, added: "I don't suppose she'll be back before Monday, but you haven't a thing to worry about, Mr Jones. My typing's super now, and as long as you don't go too fast, I can take dictation."

With a tenderly appreciative smile he examined her from

natural blonde hair to open-toed sandals, the certainty that there was nothing in the world she would not do for him, a sore temptation. Self-righteously he put it behind him.

"Fine. Where's the post?"

"On your desk. And when you want a cup of coffee, you've only to ring, Mr Jones. Any time."

"It's a bit like being let out of school, isn't it?" he teased, and she glowed back at him.

Vanessa lacked Mrs Wisley's symmetry. He had to sort through a sprawling mound before he came on the envelope he'd warned himself might be there. Shielding it from Vanessa's glance that would be pivoted in his direction all day, he examined the date-stamp. Crumley, 4.25 P.M. Wednesday. Which meant that any member of the Red Man's band of spies could have put it in either of the two post-boxes after 9.40 when the morning collection was made. Tony? Hexham? Norris? Mrs Wisley? Or Sam Goodsell scuttling out of sight last night, looking as guilty as sin itself! He ripped the envelope open.

Shorter this time. Two neatly inscribed lines of block lettering:

KEEP WATCH. I AM
SO'S DARLING DADDY.

His reaction to it was the same as to the other two: puerile scribbling, the by-product of a child-mind lodged in an adult body, giggling convulsively: "Ha, ha! I know something you don't!" Only he or she plainly didn't know anything except that he was the Red Man's bonded serf—so was intent on rubbing salt into the wound of his humiliation. But the laugh was on them, wasn't it, because now the end of his servitude was in sight, and after Sunday no one would be able to jeer. Once the Red Man was dead, he'd line up his suspects, exact a penalty that would make him or her squirm and beg for mercy. Meantime, he put the card in his wallet to keep the other two company.

He did not catch sight of Curtis until Vanessa tripped forward to receive him. He gestured her away, came plodding towards the door of Ashley's glass box.

"Morning," Ashley said. "What can I do for you? I hope it won't take too long. We're short-staffed this morning. But come in, sit down."

Curtis refused, explained politely he had brought Mr Jones a simple request from Superintendent Ross. Would he be good enough to accompany him back to headquarters?

"Sorry, quite impossible." With a gesture Ashley indicated Vanessa. "I can hardly leave the saleroom in sole charge of a teen-age girl."

That, Sergeant Curtis intimated, was Ashley's problem. Unmoved by argument or persuasion, he further hinted that should Ashley prove unco-operative, the request would be enforced in a manner he was not, at the moment, prepared to divulge.

At Helton Police station Ashley was assured that Superintendent Ross would not keep him long, shown into a waiting-room. One table was pushed against a porridge-coloured wall, another stood in the centre of the room. There were a few ill-used looking chairs, a free-standing chromium ash-tray, and bending over it a woman smoking in a manner to suggest that she was suffering from a bout of shaky nerves.

Automatically Ashley ran an eye over her. Middle-aged, stringy, wearing an assortment of singularly ill-matched garments, bare legs, feet with repulsive protruding joints breaking out of dirty white sandals. He turned away, and tried to calculate what, if any, menace lay behind the summons from Ross. What nugget of fact or fiction had he uncovered? Nothing, he assured himself, that couldn't be argued into the ground. Reaching to drop his spent match in the chromium ash-tray, he found the woman's slightly bloodshot eyes glued to his face. Damn it, he *had* seen her somewhere or other. In a shop? A pub? On the other side of a restaurant? He decided the last label fitted best. She looked the type, had the broken feet that were an occupational hazard for all waitresses. He was turning over whether it was worth the effort of drawing her into conversation to confirm that his guess was right, when the door was half-opened and, anticipating a summons from Ross, he glanced towards it questioningly.

But it was shut from the outside on a tall, lank-figured man with a crop of bright silver hair, who would have possessed a claim to distinction if his face, gouged with lines and furrows, hadn't been balanced by what could only be animal fright.

There was an interlude of strained silence as Ashley and the woman bent their united gazes upon him, before the door opened again, and a policeman beckoned imperatively towards the woman. She jumped up, scurried out so fast that she lost a sandal and, swearing under her breath, had to stoop to retrieve it.

As the door clicked shut, the man collapsed rather than sat down on the nearest chair. Ashley strolled forward, offered his cigarette case. "Are you here to see Superintendent Ross?"

The man shook his head in dumb negation, didn't appear to notice the proffered cigarettes.

Could be, Ashley conjectured, that he was suffering from the shock of waking up to find that his car, his dog, even his wife had disappeared. Could be, but such a degree of inner disturbance rendered it unlikely. Anyway, it was worth a question. "I wonder were you by any chance a friend of Monica Price?"

The man jumped to his feet in a spasm so violent that the chair flew backwards, as he shouted in fury: "Mind your own damned business. Who the hell are you? What right have you to ask me questions?"

Before Ashley could reply, the door opened again and a policeman said invitingly: "If you'd come this way, Mr Jones, Superintendent Ross is free to see you now."

Both Ross's eyes, the one that was fully exposed, and the other that was slightly shielded from view by the dipping lid, directed a look of implacable, tight-clenched anger at Ashley as, without being invited to do so, he nonchalantly took the chair on the other side of the desk.

"Mr Jones, I'm about to ask you some straight, simple questions. You'd be very ill-advised to feed me with a fresh supply of lies." He nodded to Curtis, who opened his notebook.

Ross jabbed a nicotine-stained finger at a line in the bound book lying open on his desk. "This entry . . ."

But Ashley was ahead of him, had already recognised it for what it was: a hotel register. Bad luck! It had always been a marginal risk. Obviously the woman outside had been employed at the hotel or, more likely, was the proprietor's wife. What he'd been submitted to was a rigged-up identity parade. He wondered if it were entirely legal. And where did the chalk-faced zombie come in? Before he could pursue that line of speculation, Ross threw the date at him. He and Monica had registered as Mr and Mrs Price, for the two nights had occupied a double room. "She was your mistress, a fact you took pains to conceal from me. Why?"

"Simple," Ashley replied with a disarming assumption of virtue. "My motives were so commendable that I don't even feel I owe you an apology. I lied to protect the reputation of a close friend who had died in the most appallingly distressing circumstances. It was perfectly evident to me that you'd already decided from all the rumours you'd taken down in your little notebooks that she was a Scarlet Woman. I didn't want . . ."

Ross broke in savagely: "This wasn't a rumour. It was documented fact. Why did you register in her name, not yours?"

"Jones!" he exclaimed in heavy irony. "Only one degree better than Mr and Mrs Smith! Very suspect. Monica couldn't have cared less."

And then, inevitably, he was subjected to a hammering of questions. How long had he and Monica been lovers? When had the affair begun? When had it ended? Why had it ended? Had they quarrelled? If so, over what?

With an air that he was exercising superhuman patience under brutal and indefensible bullying, Ashley coolly provided the answers. The affair had lasted eight or nine months. It hadn't ended for any specific reason; it had merely, like most affairs, faded out by mutual consent. No hard feelings on either side.

Back practically to the day he was born, advancing tediously but not particularly painfully to the 30th of May two years ago. At that point Ashley leaned on the device of trying to recall his movements on the Sunday following The Sunday. It served him well because he couldn't, in all honesty, remember what he'd done.

Then Ross began harping on the money. Monica had been blackmailing him, threatening that if he did not pay her £2,000 she would go to his fiancée, lay before her in irrefutable detail the facts of their relationship. £2,000! That God-almighty Ross had got his sums wrong lent an extra-skin of imperturbability to Ashley's denials.

Suddenly Ross leaned forward, opened his fist, spread it under Ashley's gaze. "I'm right in assuming this is yours, aren't I?"

Ashley stared blankly at the pocket-sized pearl-handled fruit knife with a hinged blade that was islanded in Ross's none too clean palm. "You're wrong. It's not mine."

Ross went on as if he hadn't heard: "A pretty piece. It didn't drop out of the sky, you know. Someone sold it across a counter. Someone else bought it, probably gave it away as a present."

Ashley shook his head affably. "As you say, a pretty piece, if rather the worse for wear. I feel I owe you an apology because it hasn't got my initials engraved on the silver panel. But it hasn't, has it?"

"If it had, what would they have been: H.R.H. or D.D.?"

He had to fight hard to keep his smile in place, the tremor of shock from showing in his hands that were under Ross's eye. The uncontrollable blink of surprise wouldn't count against him: it was the natural reaction to a meaningless question.

"I don't follow you," he said in a slightly bored voice. "Ashley Jones. A.J. Not even a middle name."

"What about a nick-name by which Monica Price called you? She didn't always address you by your Christian name, did she?"

"Darling," he suggested. "A.D. there. Nothing else that I can recall."

When the inevitable moment of stalemate arrived Ross barked in the tone of a man long past the breaking-point of endurance: "Okay, Mr Jones. That's all for the moment. I've no doubt we'll be seeing one another again. Sergeant Curtis will type out a statement for you to sign, and meanwhile I take it you'll have no objection to having your fingerprints taken?"

"Would it make any difference if I did?"

Ross's reply was to beckon to Curtis to take him away. By the time the statement was ready to sign, he'd beaten down his alarm to manageable proportions. The statement contained no new evidence against him except that nearly a year before she was murdered he and Monica had stayed two nights at the Ferncliffe Hotel. Hardly incriminating! And fingerprints, even supposing any were left on the car, could be old ones . . . The little trick of Ross with the toy-knife? He shrugged that one off.

So what was left to badger him into a sense of chaos breaking about him? Three initials. H.R.H. Had Monica ever used that taunting name in public? If so, who had overheard, preserved it to whisper in Ross's ear. Or had she written it down somewhere? The possibility set alarm roaring in his head. In her handbag they'd have found in the car, or what portions of it hadn't rotted away? But paper would have disintegrated . . . It couldn't still exist. Even so, he cursed himself for not anticipating the act of God that had exposed her bones to the police. Forewarned of that danger he'd have burnt her handbag instead of wedging it in the glove compartment of the car.

It was the purchase of the two small tools required for Saturday night, made at widely spaced shops in Helton, that put the gathering cloud of doubts to rout. Initials were all Ross had been able to produce, not the actual name. He was hawking round a set of three letters desperately trying to pin them on somebody. For a fleeting moment he remembered the man with the furrowed face, nerves shot to hell in the waiting-room. What was *his* name?

Seated in the chair that Ashley had vacated, Richard Price spoke in a voice given authority by the calm he had managed to impose upon it before entering the room. "I wish to lodge a protest. You are at liberty to ask me what you like, but I will not allow you to badger my wife. You have no right to . . ."

Ross interrupted sharply: "On the contrary, Mr Price, as an officer of the law in charge of a murder enquiry, I have a right to question whom I please. It appears that you omitted to mention my visit of last evening to Mrs Price."

"Why should I?"

"If you had," Ross said disregarding the question, "she might not have been so distressed when I telephoned her after you'd left for your office this morning. And if you hadn't lied to me last evening, Mr Price, I'd probably have had no reason to question her. But you did, didn't you, so I had to discover for myself whether her memory was less defective than yours. Are you with me?"

"I'm afraid not."

"Then allow me to explain. Your wife clearly recalls that on the particular weekend we discussed, the last in May, two years ago, she was away from home. On the Friday, May twenty-eighth, accompanied by your daughter, she travelled by train to Reading to be with her mother who'd suddenly been taken ill. On Monday, May thirty-first, Mrs Harris was admitted to hospital. She died on Tuesday, June first. You don't dispute those dates, do you, Mr Price?"

"They are correct."

"Your wife was an only child of a widowed mother. Naturally she was upset by her mother's sudden death. You must have shared your wife's grief. Yet, last night, when I questioned you about that particular weekend, you did not recall the fact that during it Mrs Harris was taken seriously ill, died two days later? I find that odd, Mr Price."

"I don't recall any question concerning the date of her death."

Ross jabbed angrily: "You were alone during that weekend, Mr Price. Have you any sort of alibi for Sunday May thirtieth as proof that you didn't drive via the route supplied you by Monica Price to Keeper's Cottage, murder her?"

"No alibi," Richard said reasonably, "except presumably there has to be a motive for murder, and I had none."

"Hadn't you," Ross said menacingly. "Wasn't your former wife blackmailing you for a sum of money which you had, before Mrs Harris died and you were promoted to your present job, no means of obtaining?"

"No," Richard said, and added with an air of weariness: "For the last time, Superintendent, my former wife was not blackmailing me. I did not murder her."

With a sudden movement, Ross opened a drawer, lifted out the small pearl-handled knife. "Is this yours, Mr Price? A present from your wife, your little daughter, maybe? It looks very like the kind of present a little girl might give her father?"

With an effort that drew on the last remnant of his self-control, Richard brought his glance to meet Ross's. "It is not mine, but it does happen to be identical with one I have at home. And yes, my daughter did give it to me, one Christmas."

"Which Christmas?"

"I don't remember. Some while ago."

"And you're sure it is still in your possession."

"Quite sure. Why do you want to know?"

"Because we found this one in your former wife's grave."

"It was probably hers."

"Or it dropped out of the pocket of the man who murdered her."

Richard tried to smile, was proud that he succeeded. "That's your guess, isn't it?"

"Yes. Would you, Mr Price, now be prepared to hazard a guess as to the owners of the two sets of initials I mentioned to you last night? D.D. and H.R.H."

"I'm afraid not. I've never known anyone to whom either of them could apply," and knew as he said the last word that his powers of deception were crumbling away. If he were held another minute . . .

But he wasn't. With a request that he allow his finger-prints to be taken, wait until the statement he'd made had been typed, signed, Ross dismissed him.

He got into his car, with roughly an hour in which to rehearse his answers to Sylvie's questions. Not too difficult, except that to convince her past a single fluttering doubt that he was speaking the truth, he had to believe it himself.

Chapter 11

On Saturday morning Hexham, as always, woke on the stroke of five. The sun, already flowing in strength through the window over which he had pulled back the curtains before getting into bed, spotlighted the small suitcase set on the chest of drawers, the noses of its four corners battered to snubness. It contained the bare essentials for an overnight stay, plus two paper-backs, and a box of Turkish delight that, when he'd last visited her, had been his mother's favourite sweetmeat. She had no telephone, and his offer to supply her with one had been spurned, so he'd be forced to send her a telegram. "Emergency here regret unable get away. Letter follows. Love Roger."

The excuse for Meg? A guest had arrived unexpectedly to occupy his mother's only spare room. Alternatively his mother had been called to the bedside of a sick friend. Others came glibly to his tongue, but none with a solid enough ring of conviction to thwart Meg's determination to launch him forth on a weekend's rest cure. He could hear her arguing back. "But you don't have to stay with your mother, Mr Hexham. Go to an hotel, anywhere that'll give you a change from work, an uninterrupted night's sleep."

Dogged, in some ways undefeatable, like her father, and,

where her deepest emotions were concerned, blind in mind if not in sight, and stone-deaf.

The day's schedule was that he would leave Laburnum Lodge in time to catch the 1.30 London train, return by the one arriving at Crumley station at 10.40 on Sunday night. But it was a plan overhung with a query because he still wasn't sure that when he set his steps in the required direction his feet would obey him.

He lay turning over in his head the disturbing incident of yesterday evening when he'd found an automatic pistol stowed away under a pile of handkerchiefs in the top drawer of Mr Gasson's bedside cabinet. He could still hear the echo of the shout that had blasted his ear-drums when he'd opened the drawer to tidy away the protruding lid of a cigar box: "You damned interfering fool. Take your hands out of there. From now on it's private."

He'd closed the drawer instantly, made no comment. But Mr Gasson had known what he'd seen, challenged him to admit it with a hard, hating glance, as the laboured breath heaved through his lungs.

When he'd taken up his duties at Laburnum Lodge, after expounding on the patient's case-history, Dr Pratt had gone on to deliver a tacit warning against a suicide attempt, pointed out that Frederick Gasson's temperament was both mercurial and excessively violent, that for nearly a year he had existed on a see-saw of hope that, for the moment, was suspended if not abandoned. He had demanded that the eminent London consultants should put him on his feet, get his legs walking. When they'd failed, he'd been stubbornly unco-operative in their efforts to alleviate his plight by physiotherapy, a steel-jacket, a specially constructed wheelchair.

"So," Dr Pratt had finished, "you can imagine the purgatory for a man who, as far as his home ground is concerned, used to regard his word as absolute law? I don't have to say any more, do I?"

Hexham said no. Until now, though he'd automatically kept a check on drugs, sharp knives, any glass that could easily be smashed, he had not considered a suicide attempt by his patient a valid possibility. But a pistol so pointedly near his hand! Dressed, he walked softly into Mr Gasson's room. He was still asleep, unlikely to wake until around six. It would be a simple exercise for him, trained in noiseless movement, stealthily to confiscate the pistol while Mr Gasson slept. But what happened when he woke, almost certainly checked that the gun was still there?

If it wasn't loaded, constituted no menace, what right had he to appropriate what might be no more than a sentimental relic of his youth, send him into a fury of justifiable resentment, the debilitating effect of which would last for days, impose an extra burden on Meg—always supposing he went away?

Plainly the pistol had been packed in the box that he'd been ordered to bring out of the dining-room, stow away unopened. But who had lifted the box out of the drawer, untied the knots, disposed of box and cord? It could have been any one of five visitors who'd spent time alone with Mr Gasson since Wednesday morning: Dr Pratt, Mr Hodkins, the solicitor who'd paid a second visit on Thursday afternoon bringing documents for signature, Mr Tyson from the Bank, and Mr West and old Sam Goodsell both of whom had been closeted with him on Wednesday evening.

Having decided that the most sensible course was to consult Dr Pratt when he paid his usual Saturday morning visit, he went into the kitchen to make himself early tea.

Looking up from the ironing board, Meg laughed at his visible start of surprise. "I know, for once I'm up with the birds!" She was wearing a clean white shirt over a pair of faded blue jeans, no make-up, and her hair pulled back, tied with a ribbon on the top of her head. He thought that a stranger would have guessed her age at around nineteen.

"It's my big day as well as yours, so I decided to get the laundry away before breakfast, not get in an unholy flap because I have to drive into Helton to have a hair-do while Elsie is here to mind Pip." She rubbed a crick in her back. "While you're at it, make a pot for both of us and I'll take a ten-minute break."

Sitting by his side at the table, cup held aloft in both hands, she said hesitantly: "Mr Hexham, you don't hold a grudge against me because I bullied you into going away, do you?"

"Of course I don't. Any bullying you did was done out of consideration for me." Because she continued to look unconvinced, he smiled, added with an attempt at lightness: "You're like your father. You don't take no for an answer, do you?"

Her reaction was to cry out: "You've got such a wonderful smile, Mr Hexham. I think that's what's worried me most about you: you hardly ever smile." She leaned her head slightly to one side, suddenly a little shy. "Why are you such a sad person? What happened to you?"

"You mean," he said with a sting of dismay, "that I'm bad-tempered?"

"Heavens, no. I've never known anyone with a nicer disposition, kinder. It's just that you look what I've just said: sad."

Once or twice he'd indulged himself in a daydream wherein he admitted her to his past, visualising it as a momentous occasion, fraught with consequences that might destroy their strange, uneven relationship. But in reality there was no drama, no emotion except for the healing ease that came from telling the right person at the right moment.

"If I look sad maybe it's because in prison you grow a sort of mental skin, grey, drab. Even after you come out, it sticks, makes you feel and act differently from other people. Perhaps you never lose it entirely . . . I can't know yet."

"Prison!" she spoke the word without shock, but with muted pity that stole strength from her voice.

"Criminal carelessness while in charge of a car. The one I was driving killed three people: my father, my young sister, another woman."

"An accident!" She stared at him, compassion fighting horror. "An accident and they sent you to prison?"

"The car wasn't insured. It was an old jalopy I'd borrowed from a friend while I was in my second year Medical School. He forgot to tell me the insurance had run out; I forgot to check. I came home for the weekend and because Dad's car was in dock, I taxied the family around. It happened when I was driving Elaine and Dad home from a party. I thought I'd room to overtake, but when the crunch came it wasn't there. It was a head-on crash." He closed his eyes in a futile attempt to erect a barrier against a horror picture that never faded. "I wasn't drunk, but I'd had sufficient alcohol in my blood content for it to count against me."

Rhythmically, without being aware she was doing it, she stroked his arm, comforting him as if he had been Pip, who'd tumbled, hurt himself.

After a moment she got up, poured away the cups of tea that had cooled, poured fresh ones.

"Mr Hexham, why didn't you go back to Medical School after you came out of prison, become a doctor?"

"My father, quite naturally, hadn't expected to die at fifty. He had no life insurance, no pension. We lived in a rented house. The result was that my mother not only found herself a widow but penniless. If the Medical School would have re-admitted me—and I don't know that they would have—it would have been four years before I'd been able to help her financially."

"But surely," she protested hotly, "someone would have come to your rescue, tided you over, stopped the waste. Nobody's that alone!"

His smile flicked on and off nervously. "I'm not sure I wanted to go back. Self-inflicted penance, or pure funk that I wouldn't be able to get back into the rhythm of swotting, fail my finals? If I'm honest it was probably a mixture of both. Also when you smash your life down to the foundation, have to begin to build it from the ground up, it's safest to plan one that's simple, easy to manage, that's unlikely to be subjected to the stress of risk."

"But you never get anywhere if you don't take a risk." She smiled at him all over her face. "There I go, being bossy again! Forgive me, and thank you for telling me, Mr Hexham. I'm sorry . . . I wish it hadn't happened to you."

One of Ashley's few victories over the Red Man had been to secure for himself a five-and-a-half-day working week, won with the aid of Meg's insistence that she had a right to her husband's company on Saturday afternoon. As a result, when the works closed at 12.30 Tom Norris donned collar and tie, his good suit, became Regent-in-Charge of the saleroom for the afternoon.

Friday had brought no sniping card either to home or office. None was on Ashley's desk that morning. A clear pointer of guilt in Mrs Wisley's direction, now incapacitated to such a degree she couldn't hold a pen in her hand?

And dead silence on the Ross front, sure proof that his cunningly erected set-piece at Helton Police station on Thursday had tumbled round his ears. That evening the Red Man had glowered vitriolic hate all over him but, curiously, had made no reference to Ross's peremptory summons, a report on which must have reached him via Tony at noon. Neither, it seemed, had he raged at Meg because she'd married a man at whom the police were pointing fingers of suspicion. If he had, she would have passed on the message; instead of which she hadn't mentioned Ross. So he felt safe in assuming there was general alarm and despondency on the enemy front.

After a pleasant but harmless parting exchange with Vanessa, he left his gold-fish bowl on Saturday lunchtime, riding so high on a sense of jubilation that he was insulated against a jab of alarm at the sight of Sergeant Trent showing Curtis and presumably a fellow detective into a parked police car, their glances lingering on him until he was out of sight. It was The Day. His Day of Vengeance, nothing could mar.

As a precaution because the morning's post had not arrived until after he'd left, he scanned the hall table for letters—none were visible—before he deposited the morning's report, scabby with Vanessa's rubbings out, on the Red Man's bed. His final act of penance! In celebration he did not even pause for a nod of dismissal, went straight out into the hall. Meg came running to him. Her hair was confined in a net, her nose was shining, and, as always, when she was agitated, she gabbled.

"I'm sorry, darling, but lunch will be late. I'd got the whole day planned out beautifully, and then at the hairdresser's Jean went and threw me out by keeping me waiting over half an hour. Really . . ."

He broke across the stream of words. "Any letters for me?"

It wasn't a question he normally asked, and she blinked in surprise. "Yes, I remember now, there was one. I put it somewhere." At the hiss of scalding water meeting a hotplate she turned her head distractedly towards the kitchen.

"I'll find it in a minute, but something's boiling over. Just a second . . ."

When she came back her hands were empty, but she was wearing the smile she put on when she was about to beg a favour. "Darling, I can't possibly have lunch ready for twenty minutes, so could you run Hexham to the station? His train goes at 1.30, and it's much too hot to walk fast."

Before he had time to answer, Hexham came through the second door of his room that opened into the back of the hall. "Thank you, Mrs Jones, but there's no need. I've plenty of time to walk. I've been waiting to see Dr Pratt. I wanted a word with him."

Meg clapped a hand to her mouth in dismay. "I forgot to tell you. Mrs Pratt telephoned to say he'd been called out to Ellison's farm; a bad tractor accident. He's got an urgent baby-case too, so she explained he wouldn't get round to Daddy until after tea. I'm sorry, I should have told you. Why did you want to see him? Is something worrying you?"

Ashley interrupted: "Is something wrong with Mr Gasson?"

"Not wrong," Hexham said looking at Meg, "but I did want to speak to Dr Pratt."

Ashley reached forward, took the suitcase out of his grasp. "Surely it'll keep till you see him on Monday. Shall we get going?"

Hexham said stiffly: "Mr Jones, I'd prefer not to trouble you. I've plenty of time to walk."

"You have not," Meg said severely. "You've left it too late, and I'm not going to risk you missing your train." She held out her hand. "And, to please me, have a good time."

Outside Ashley gunned the car, yelled: "Hexham!"

It might have been cutting it fine to walk, but there was an over-allowance of time for the drive. When they ran over the level crossing it was only fifteen minutes past one, the train not even signalled.

In the station yard, Ashley turned to take a final look at the Red Man's top spy before he became unemployed. Now his potential for harm was reduced to nil, he cut such a pitiful figure that Ashley scoffed at himself for the harassment and frustration he'd allowed Hexham to inflict on him. Well, all behind him now, so he could afford a semblance of affability. As the train made two stops before Charing Cross, he enquired: "Where are you bound for?"

"London."

"Ah, bright lights!" He laughed at the absurdity of suggesting that Hexham was capable of living it up.

Hexham reached for the door handle, got out of the car. As he said goodbye, thanked Mr Jones for the lift, he thought that in addition to the dead-pan killer eyes, his smile was a give-away: self-designed, as artificial as if it had been turned out of a plastic mould.

He could feel it bearing on his back all the way to the ticket office, as he waited, nerves tensing, for a sound that did not come: the Jaguar engine in reverse. Two travellers were ahead of him at the window, and as he stood behind them he resolved that if he heard the car driving out of the yard before his turn came, he would walk away without buying a ticket. His defence? The pistol in Mr Gasson's cabinet, the failure of the police to arrest Monica Price's murderer.

When he stepped out on to the platform the slip of cardboard in his hand, he saw why the car engine had stayed silent. Ashley Jones was chatting to the solitary porter who was guffawing sycophantly at Mr Jones's wit.

As Ashley, hands in pockets, with an air of possessing the world, strolled towards him, Hexham stared into the face that, hard-glazed with ridicule, proclaimed that Ashley

Jones knew all about the torments of indecision that had racked him, the resolutions that had caved in before he could act on them.

"I thought I might as well see you into the train. My wife is sure to want to know if you got a comfortable seat. Plenty of room," he said, as the train ran into the platform. "You're going to enjoy the luxury of a carriage to yourself." He gave Hexham's elbow a thrust upwards, slammed the door on him, then stood back. "My wife," he shouted, "is anxious that you should forget all about us, have a good rest. Mind you follow her advice." When the hum of the diesel engine was sufficiently loud to drown the sound, he laughed aloud.

With Hexham gone, there remained only one small problem to be solved: to ensure that during the afternoon he had half an hour free of Meg fussing round his feet.

After parking the car in the drive, he went down to the bottom of the garden, lifted from the summer-house a foam-padded chaise longue that Meg never found time to set up for herself. He arranged it under a patch of shade, shook the cushions, adjusted the fringed canopy.

Meg exclaimed from behind him: "My, you are making careful preparations for your afternoon siesta! Sure you wouldn't like me to stand beside you and wave a palm-leaf!"

"Not my siesta. Yours. If you don't take one, you're not going to be fit for Libby's party."

She sighed. "What a heavenly idea! But I've still got a thousand things to do."

"Either I do them for you, or they get left undone. Darling, for once relax."

She said, her voice a caress: "You're so sweet. Nobody but me knows how sweet. I shouldn't, but maybe I will. Just for an hour. I was up so early."

He caught the movement of her hand towards the pocket

in her apron, asked on an urgent note he was powerless to quell: "Is that my letter?"

Instead of handing it to him, she read out disapprovingly: "'Personal and Confidential.' Who do they think opens your letters!"

Snatching it from her, he made an effort to tease. "My guess is that they're taking normal precautions against inquisitive wives."

Her expression turned mildly hurt. "Why? Who's it from?"

"Don't ask questions or you won't have a surprise for your birthday."

"My birthday! But it's ages away."

"Some presents require a lot of work beforehand."

She grinned. "Then you're not going to open it?"

"Not while you're around to peep over my shoulder." He put it away in his pocket.

She laughed. "Beast! You're probably planning to give me a present you're dying to have yourself. Did Hexham get off all right?"

"Yes. A carriage all to himself."

She said with warmth: "I'm glad. I'm sure he'll be better for a break. This morning, before you were up, for the first time he told me something about himself. It's all terribly sad . . ."

"You must tell me sometime," he said, hustling her back to the house so fast that she had no breath left to repeat whatever nauseating details of his personal history Hexham had confided to her.

By dint of exerting himself to help in the removal of dishes, plates; refusing cheese, gulping his coffee, lunch was over in thirty minutes. It was another twenty before Meg had satisfied herself that all was well with her father and Pip, and he'd got her stretched out on the chaise longue.

"I'll hear Daddy's bell from here, so all you've got to

do is listen for Pip. He'll be awake in about half an hour, but after that he's usually content to play with his toys for a bit."

"I'll cope. Now, you're sure you've got everything? The object of this enterprise is that you rest . . . not come tripping back to the house for a magazine, a cold drink."

"You're an angel," she said, closing her eyes. "I'm practically asleep already."

"That's what you're meant to be."

In the kitchen, he turned his back on the washing up, took the card out of its envelope. This time the writer had excelled in puerility.

REMEMBER THE OLD SAYING
FINDER'S KEEPERS?

For God's sake, he muttered disgustedly, a half-wit! Finder's Keepers! Keepers of what? A riddle to which there was no solution because it was meaningless twaddle concocted to sustain the writer's idiot ploy of harping on one word. A threat with nothing to back it up, an attempt to blackmail him, not for money, but to steal his nerve. And a resounding flop! So to hell with the guessing game until the Red Man was dead.

First he stationed himself in the hall, out of range of the Red Man's spy-hole through his half-open door, the cigar smoke drifting through the gap, evaporating in the air, evidence that he was awake. Then, superimposed on the purr of the electric fan, he heard the catarrhal cough that suggested, if he lived long enough—which he wouldn't—the Red Man would choke on his own phlegm.

Next, muffling the click of the door—the Red Man had ears like a hawk—he spent ten minutes among the fuse boxes. The mechanism was simple, presenting no problem. Total failure of all lighting apparatus was a side-effect cal-

culated to add confusion to chaos when, inevitably, out-
siders arrived on the scene. Treading softly upstairs, he kept
to the left-hand side, well out of the Red Man's area of
vision.

The cupboard in the bathroom was a credit to Meg's
squirrel-thrift, her congenital inability to throw anything
away. Eye and nose drops, three proprietary brands of as-
pirin, laxatives, gargles, cough and throat tablets, embroca-
tion, insect repellents, salve for burns, sticking plaster, and
rolls of bandages. He had to disarrange a miniature drug-
store before he found what he wanted. He prised off the
cap, poured the contents of the phial on to his palm. Twelve
capsules prescribed by Dr Pratt for Meg during the last
months of her pregnancy when, for the first time in her life,
she'd been unable to fall asleep the instant her head
touched the pillow. Then, having got them, she'd been
scared of their effect on her baby, never swallowed one.

He deducted three, put them in his wallet, returned the
phial to its place, packed it round with bottles and chemists'
pill-boxes.

The three farcically simple tools he required to murder
the Red Man were in his photographic cupboard in the
spare room, into which Meg never pried except once a year
at spring-cleaning. He added the last item, a pair of cotton
gloves he wore occasionally when working on the car.

All preparatory work done, until he set out to escort Meg
to the party, he experienced a sensation of anti-climax
born of his urgent yearning to reach the climax, be over the
summit, running down to the plains of rich and easy living.

Chapter 12

It was past seven when Meg and Ashley drove up to Beechgrove Farm. Dr Pratt, arriving at 5.30 had set up the first delay. Meg, left vaguely jittery by Hexham's remark, had insisted on him giving her father a thorough examination.

"Can't find any new symptom he'd want to discuss with me," Dr Pratt announced when he'd finished. "Any idea what he wanted to talk to me about, Frederick?"

"No," Frederick said shortly, and Dr Pratt took his leave, promising to look in on Monday when Hexham would be back on duty.

Then Pip turned resentful at being hustled to bed by his mother and wasn't to be pacified in a hurry; and her hair, when she tried to comb it back into its professional set, rebelled, developed a rakish will of its own.

When, finally, hot with exertion, she came downstairs, it was to find Ashley leisurely sipping sherry with Sister Melton. Nothing would suit him but she had one, and then a second because, he insisted, she still looked fraught, in no mood to enjoy a party.

"Not another for me," Sister Melton said virtuously. "I'm on duty. But you go on, Mrs Jones. Do what your husband says, relax, and don't worry about a thing; I know where everything is. I should do, you've told me enough times."

At the farm the sounds of a party running in top gear, the rich smell of roasting meat drew them towards the terrace, where they were penned back behind a jam of guests. It was a minute or two before Ian, at the barbecue pit, chef's cap awry on his head, spied them, waved vigorously to alert Libby, who disengaged herself, squeezed towards them.

"So you made it! I'm so glad. Meg, darling, how sweet you look in that dress. I'm afraid I played safe and stuck to slacks. There's always a moment when the most sedate guests throw off their inhibitions and start playing badminton with chop bones and sausages."

Meg, conscious of the gaffe she'd made in dressing for a summer cocktail party blushed crimson, replied too quickly: "Oh, it's only an old rag. If it went up in flames, I wouldn't shed a tear."

"It looks brand new to me," Libby murmured. "Now drinks. You're at least four behind the rest of us, so you'd better start catching up." She beckoned a waiter with a tray of glasses. "You may well look, hired help! That way Ian's free to concentrate on his cooking."

A visibly pregnant girl, who'd moved away from Crumley when she married, was back home visiting her parents, grabbed Meg's arm. "Meg Gasson, don't tell me you were going to cut me dead!"

As a rush of girlish chatter exploded between the two of them, Ashley and Libby moved on, pressure from the crowd keeping them side by side.

"How's everything?" Libby enquired.

He turned his head, caught what he called her feline look that managed to express both hope and hostility. "Fine. Any reason why it shouldn't be?"

"You'd know that better than I would, wouldn't you?"

He said with no resentment: "Libby, you're a prize bitch. You'd love to see me in trouble, wouldn't you?"

"Because you're too clever for your own good. One of these days you're going to fall flat on your pretty face."

She went forward more thrustfully, then turned her head, called over her shoulder: "By the way it's no good looking for your soul-mate. He's tied up in his kennel in the stables. But enjoy yourself, and don't forget to look after Meg. I'd hate her to go home hungry."

He did so, never better, not because Libby had asked him to, but because the party was the curtain raiser to the best conjuring trick of all time. Thursday, he'd decided, was the likeliest day for the Red Man's funeral. And on that morning, the sleeping dream of himself, standing in the hall, head bowed, heart aburst with jubilation, watching the coffin borne to the hearse, would be taken out from the close seclusion of his brain, be brought four-squarely to life.

It was ten minutes past eleven when, after slipping away to feed three half-consumed lamb chops to Prince, Ashley merged back into the crowd on the floodlit lawn, heard Tony saying at his elbow with that air of jesting he always found suspect: "For a hard-drinking man, you seem to be having a remarkably abstemious evening."

Ashley, damning his spying pop-eyes, bounced the joke back at him. "Why, have you been keeping count?"

Tony shrugged. "Merely a general observation."

"A waste of a good party, surely, keeping a tag on some-one else's drinks instead of one's own!" He reached for a half-full glass he'd parked on the edge of a teak garden table before he'd made his trip to the stables. Sipping from it, he held Tony under close scrutiny. Beneath the skin of good-humour, the air he invariably adopted at any gathering of being a star guest, did he detect a hint of nerves tightening? Due to frustration, to hope being deferred so long it was beyond hailing distance?

He smiled, said: "By the way that crystal ball of yours went a little haywire, didn't it? I mean about your hero Ross being about to clap a suspect in irons?"

Tony snapped: "I never said that."

"You didn't! Then I must have misunderstood you." For a long moment he looked at the line of the mouth that had turned peevish, said experimentally on the jump of an irresistible impulse: "Finder's Keepers, eh?"

Tony blinked. "What the devil do you mean?"

Surprise, bafflement certainly, but weren't both a mite overdone? Tony exploiting an immature sense of humour —he'd always been given to infantile practical jokes— abetted by his natural vengeful spite? Could be. The style of printing . . . wouldn't Sam Goodsell's or Norris's block letters have been more painstakingly drawn? And Mrs Wisley, unless she'd co-opted her husband or a neighbour, hadn't been in Crumley to post the last card. Tony, he decided with pleasurable certainty, was the most likely suspect. When the inevitable high drama of tomorrow's resulting pandemonium was behind him, say on Monday morning, he would spread the four cards out on the desk under Tony's ugly pug-nose, force a confession out of him. If he wasn't the culprit, Hexham came next on the list. At long range he tossed him a jeer: an involuntary exile from Laburnum Lodge. Probably asleep, and if so, undoubtedly dreaming lustfully of Meg. That Hexham was in some freakish, perverted fashion in love with his wife had been apparent to Ashley for months. Not that Meg noticed, or was likely to. Married and a mother she still remained the personification of sexual innocence.

As if the passage of her name across his thoughts had charmed her out of space, she materialised at his shoulder, leaned heavily against it, groaned: "Darling, something awful's happened. I'm tight. I think I'd better go home."

"Tight!" He laughed the idea to scorn. "You don't know the meaning of the word. You're just nicely lit up. We'll go as soon as Ian has put a match to his fireworks. His set-piece is a cow . . . presumably the one that won the prize. It would break his heart if we didn't watch. Look, there he is down there . . ."

Tony dragged a chair forward, eased Meg into it. "Silly girl! I don't suppose it's the amount you've drunk, but what. Aren't you old enough to know you can't mix your drinks!"

Mournfully Meg, ignoring the firework display, rubbed a grease stain on her dress, a ladder that was creeping up her leg, wailed: "I've never been to a barbecue before. Someone should have warned me what goes on."

"No harm done," Ashley said cheeringly. "The dress will clean and I'll buy you half a dozen pairs of new nylons on Monday."

She blinked in an attempt to persuade her eyes to focus, but even so couldn't see the time by her wrist-watch. A reeling in her head, a combination of self-pity and embarrassment turned her voice maudlin. "You're my angel boy, but you know we have to be home by half-past eleven. We promised Sister Melton we wouldn't be late. Ashley, please, darling, I want to go . . ."

He took her away, making a great play of having to hold her upright. Everyone who saw their exit considered it the high-spot of the evening: like the head-prefect disgracing herself.

Inside Laburnum Lodge Meg clung to the hall table in an effort to steady her knees, as Sister Melton, face blurred under the uniform hat that her patients swore she never took off except in bed, hurried forward. With careful articulation Meg enquired: "Has everything been all right?"

"As rain," Sister Melton answered merrily. "Not a peep out of the cherub, and your father's been in the land of nod for a good hour. There was nothing on the telly but a load of old rubbish, so I amused myself by rinsing out Pip's clothes. I'll be on my way then. No, you're not to come out, Mr Jones. You both get to bed. See you in the morning about ten. Ta-ta. Sweet dreams."

When the door slammed behind her, Ashley said: "I'm going to have a night-cap. What about you?"

Meg squeezed her face in revulsion. "Not me. I'm off alcohol for life. But I *am* thirsty." Tentatively she released her grip on the table, grabbed at it again. "I've got to go upstairs to look at Pip, get my night things . . . Oh, Ashley, I feel so dizzy and such a fool."

Ashley locked an arm round her waist. "I'll fetch them, and take a look at Pip. You get straight into bed."

In order not to risk disturbing the Red Man, he guided her to the outer door of Hexham's room that opened into the lobby outside the kitchen. From the threshold, he took his first good look at it: a cell, or the de-personalised room of a nursing home readied for a new patient. Hexham had arrived to occupy it a few weeks after he and Meg had been married, yet there wasn't a single article to mark his ownership. Presumably his white coats hung in the wardrobe, his underwear lay in the drawers, but without a sight of them it was easy to imagine Hexham did not exist, had been no more than a phantom terror into which he'd breathed life.

As Meg sank on the bed, hands pressed against her eyes to shield them from the light, he exhorted: "Lie still, darling. No need to fuss: I'll see to everything."

He confirmed that Pip was sleeping, grabbed her nightwear, went down to the kitchen. Taking the pills from his wallet, he decided to revise the dosage. The effect of the alcohol Meg had consumed had been more powerful than he'd calculated. She must be doped, but not over-doped, a state that might arouse suspicion, set off a plague of enquiries. He flushed one pill down the sink, ground the other two to powder, mixed them in milk, squirted soda, then fixed a double Scotch for himself.

He propped her against his arm, held the glass to her lips. "What is it?" she asked, slurring her words.

"Milk and soda. It'll quench your thirst, stop the hangover."

She drank, grimaced. "That soda must be flat. How's Pip?"

"Asleep." He undid the zipper in her dress, unhooked her bra, slid the nightdress over her head, while in slow motion she kicked off stockings, panties. When he opened the sheets, she flopped inside, closed her eyes.

He was nearly out of the room when she reared up, called out in a stone-cold sober voice: "Ashley, you've forgotten to open the doors, this one and the bathroom one. I shan't be able to hear Daddy if he calls out."

"He's got his bell. You'll hear that."

"I know, but I want the doors open. Sometimes, in the dark, he can't find his bell." She began struggling to disentangle her legs from the sheets.

"You stay there. I'll do it." When, having opened both doors, he passed the foot of the bed, she held out her arms to him in a travesty of sensual yearning. "Darling, would you have any objection to kissing a drunken wife good night?"

He did so, and to his enormous relief she subsided back on the pillow with a silly, tipsy giggle. This time, to make sure she didn't erupt into sobriety, he waited until she was asleep.

After he'd rinsed both glasses, he paused for a moment in the hall, massaging his hands lightly one within the other, like a pianist before a concert performance. Going upstairs, he switched off each light as he came to it, so it wasn't until he turned off the one on the landing that he was pitch-forked into violent shock by the disparity between the scene as he'd imagined it and its living counterpart. In the former the background had been as uniformly dark as the inside of a well, lit only intermittently and in widely separated areas by the pin-prick beam of his torch. In the second the landing was aswim with a phosphorescent glow that re-vealed every object within sight. For all the cover it gave him, he might as well have gone about what he had to do in broad daylight. He stared through the high uncurtained landing window at the great globe of the full moon, and cursed aloud all acts of God, like droughts and changing lunar phases of which no man could be expected to take account.

Felled by the unexpectedness of the silvery radiance, his breath rasped in his throat. Then he shook his head, set about re-establishing his confidence. Light or dark, it made no difference. In the nerve-centre of the whole operation, the Red Man's bedroom, the curtains would be close drawn. It would be dark enough there.

As resolutely as if there had been no searing moment of disruption, he bent to his first task which was to lay out in an exact sequence of priorities the normal man's reac-tions to catastrophe. Women and children first! In his case one wife, one child. Wouldn't a loving father's natural in-stinct propel him first to the rescue of a helpless sleeping infant, remove it from harm? So, Pip to be grabbed from his cot, rolled in blankets, borne to the place of safety he'd picked: the greenhouse.

Second Meg. Drag her, made insensible and unco-operative by over-indulgence in alcohol from her bed, lay her beside her child, an operation that would take longer, and the exact calculation of timing was crucial. If his rescue of her were over-precipitate, there was a risk that when, Meg safe, he made his 999 call, the Red Man might not be beyond resuscitation when the ambulance arrived. He'd have to play that item in programming by ear.

He undressed, put on pyjamas, but not slippers or dressing-gown; either betokened wasted seconds and under the inevitable police enquiry tomorrow—would Ross conduct it?—he must not appear to have squandered one.

He rumpled the bed, dinted one pillow, laid sheet, the one light blanket in a trail across the floor, suggesting to any busybody officer of the law who felt it encumbent upon him to examine the room, that they had fallen from his shoulders as he'd raced blindly to the rescue of wife and child.

From the spare room he collected the pencil torch he'd still need for the mechanics of disconnecting the fuses, his gloves, and the cigar and a box of matches bought in Helton of the brand used by the Red Man. Then he sat down in an easy chair by the window, cut and lit the cigar.

Nothing to do now but wait for his self-appointed deadline: one o'clock, a nerve-testing interlude in which he had to steel himself to patience. It was nearly at an end when he was jerked to his feet by three closely overlapping sounds: a car stopping at the end of the drive, the slam of a door, the car starting up again. For all the world as if a passenger had been set down at Laburnum Lodge.

From the spare room window that overlooked the drive, he searched through each of the solid blocks of shadow laid down by trees and shrubs. No moving object disarranged their natural outlines. The obvious answer denounced his jitteriness: the car had not stopped at Laburnum Lodge, but at the house immediately opposite where there was a family of teen-agers, dropped off a girl or boy coming home from a late dance.

On the landing, impatience to begin was so all-conquering, that he could not bring himself to wait out the last five minutes. But before he moved into action, he composed himself to mental and physical stillness, willing his mind to record each passing second of the next hour so that, this time, not one should be encapsuled in darkness, lost to him.

He was descending, taking each downward step with calculated deliberation when, out of space, as plainly as if he were mounting the stairs towards him, Ross exploded out of the white radiance. He stared blenched with shock, hate and fear combining in a crescendo of panic, at the long thin nose, yellowy skin, slightly hooded right eye, above the bull-dog set of the heavy shoulders, and almost screamed aloud as his shocked heart gave a mighty bound in his breast. The next moment he drove himself towards a feat that drained the energy from his limbs, sapped his last drop of moral courage, and walked straight through Ross.

He was still shaking at the horrific betrayal of reason when he dealt with the fuses. It was only when he'd tested the efficacy of his handiwork by switching on the hall light, and found it stayed dark, that he regained the calm that had been his upstairs. An apparition! Ross, wherever he was, most assuredly wasn't inside Laburnum Lodge!

In the Red Man's bedroom the drawn curtains formed a barrier against the moonlight, except for two bright hands that slipped in from the hall. One of them spread itself slantwise over the Red Man's head, the dome of his belly, arms as stiffly pinioned to his sides as if he were already laid out for burial. Only a corpse didn't snore.

He explored the top of the bedside cabinet for the onyx ash-tray, lifted it in slow motion so that there should be no chink. Clean, no doubt wiped out by Sister Melton. He rubbed it over with the butt of the three-quarter smoked cigar.

And a box of matches which might or might not have been there. Frequently, when her father had smoked his daily ration of cigars, Meg confiscated them when she said good night. Sister Melton might have done so, but she hadn't, and when catechised would be honour-bound—Sister Melton was a living embodiment of a woman who could not tell a lie—to admit it. So the box he'd bought in Helton could stay in his pyjama pocket, be disposed of later.

The prone figure of his enemy snorted, coughed catarrhally, thrashed its head from side to side on the pillow, while Ashley hung back in the cover of a projecting cupboard, hardly drew breath until the rhythmic snoring started up again.

He put the ash-tray that would tell its tale to all interested parties on the floor, at the spot it could be calculated to have slid off the bed when reprehensibly, and tragically the Red Man had fallen asleep while smoking the last third of a cigar. The butt went beside it—to cover the millionth chance that there would be any fragments left for the forensic lads to monkey with.

Then, using the bed to muffle sound, he unpicked Sister Melton's masterpiece of sheet and blanket mitreing. The first three matches applied to cotton and wool alternately resulted in no more than an acrid stench of burning, short-lived wriggles of sparks that died with the spent match. In frustration he nearly wrenched his hands out of the gloves. Since there was no reason why his fingerprints should not be found on any surface within the Red Man's room, they represented a superfluity of caution, the self-imposed hallmark of a perfectionist. He would not be panicked into discarding them.

The hospital bed of painted iron was non-inflammable, the mattress latex rubber that required a burst of hot flame to set it alight. The carpet was fire-proofed man-made fibre.

Beset by impatience as strong as pain, frustration a wall against which he had to push while distracted by the high-pitched alarm bell ringing inside his head in case the Red Man might wake, a dim but expanding suspicion that the base of his whole future was caving in under him, in the turn of a second he was set free of anxiety and panic.

Actually within reach of his hand was the old-fashioned nursing chair, with a fluted walnut back—old wood with a thin veneer—which Meg often brought in to sit on while chatting to her father, and plainly outlined on its seat lay a folded newspaper that Sister Melton, after tucking the Red Man up for the night, must have left there—a lapse to which under the pressure of police questioning, she must honourably confess. Now he was as amply provided for as if he had not prohibited himself from importing any article, except matches, a cigar, into the Red Man's bedroom, most assuredly no paper, of which a scrap might conceivably survive the combustion, be miraculously preserved for the microscopic examination of a fire expert.

His exultation was barely controllable. Now a child could have set the room ablaze. All he had to do was to ease the chair forward a few inches, link it to the bed by a trailing sheet, use one match to set the newspaper alight, place the box under the mattress where it would explode under the foam rubber.

He paused only long enough to gloat over the snake of flame that set the paper curling, begin eating into the sheet, and he was gone. Time would do the rest for him.

His foot was already reaching unhurriedly for the first stair, when, although he'd been prepared for it, the Red Man's screech of frenzied terror hit him with the violence of a blow. It was loud enough to wake the dead. Only there were no dead to hear . . . no one but a drunken woman doped with sleeping pills.

Hexham got out of the car that had given him a lift from the station, thanked the young man and his girl-friend who was too sleepy to answer. His personal moment of truth struck when he had wedged himself into the black shadow thrown over the entrance to Laburnum Lodge by a giant cupressus. The sheer lunacy of his being where he was at that hour of the night almost made him turn and run for the anonymity of the high road. He was saved from flight by his ability to diagnose his own ailment: a rabid persecution complex, not on his own behalf, but on Meg's. Its cure? Proof past doubt that it was a delusion verging on lunacy.

Slipping from one shadow to the next, stripped bare of self-esteem, he was left with one grain of consolation: provided no one saw him, his night patrol would remain an act of morbid neuroticism revealed to no one but himself.

His mission was simplicity itself. He had to convince himself that Meg and her father were safe, keep watch until morning. Before anyone was stirring, he would catch the early bus into Helton, find somewhere to wash, shave. He would spend the day picnicking on one of the nearby commons. In the late evening he would catch a train to the station beyond Crumley, wait there to board the London train that would bring him to Laburnum Lodge at the appointed hour on Sunday night.

Once, cautiously plotting his approach down the drive, he imagined he caught a glimpse of Ashley's form at the window of the spare bedroom. But so briefly that he discounted it as a chimera of his overwrought senses.

When, finally, the house stood foursquare, undisturbed, before his eyes, a sigh passed his lips, as much an expression of anti-climax as relief. Had it been his honest belief that he would arrive back to find Ashley Jones had contrived an accident that would result in the murder of his father-in-law; alternatively, that Mr Gasson would manage to get hold of the pistol, commit suicide? The truthful answer was yes. The quiet, sleeping house condemned him as a sick-minded fool.

Even so, that inner, derided but unvanquished devil of suspicion drove him to make surety doubly sure. Reason was undermined by the image of the cold utterly passionless eyes of a killer, the stark fact that a girl known to Ashley Jones had been murdered. Holding the small case close to his side, never putting a foot out of the shadows generously laid upon moonswept paths and drive by trees, shrubs and boundary hedges, he patrolled the walls. Close-drawn curtains in his patient's room made his window impenetrable. But through the top vent, left open, he could hear the familiar harsh, choky breathing. Mr Gasson was asleep, and behind the window of his own room, Meg presumably slept too with a soundness that made ludicrous nonsense of his presence outside the house.

He stood outside the front door, fingering the key Meg had given him.

"I know that I'm never out when you are, Mr Hexham, but you'll feel freer, more at home, if you have your own key, don't have to ring the bell and wait on the doorstep."

Some means of death could be administered silently, in the dark. Should he insert the key in the lock, step into the hall. But suppose Meg woke, rushed out, cried astounded into fury: "Mr Hexham, what on earth are you doing here in the middle of the night. You promised me . . ."

Deprived of a truthful explanation, he couldn't summon to mind an excuse for his return that she would find remotely feasible. So his vigil must be kept outside.

He stood back, so confident now that no one was watching, that he did not even huddle into shadow. The blank face of the house showed no bead of light. His ears could detect no sound of movement within. Asleep and safe. All his manic suspicions confuted.

He was turning the corner of the house when a succession of horrifyingly blood-chilling screams tore the silence of the night to fragments, continued to smash it in the small eternity of time it took him to jam his key in the lock.

Ashley had a blanket-swatched, sleeping child cradled in his arm, when the glare of flames, the violently ascending and descending pattern of shadows rearing up the walls, suddenly ceased to be, and through the Wagnerian chorus of the Red Man's unearthly shrieks, he was assaulted by the sounds of voices that simply could not be there.

Meg's, at its most sensible pitch, saying: "Mr Hexham, I can't think what you're doing here, but none of the switches seem to work, and we've got to have light to see how badly Daddy's hurt. Could you do something about it? There are candles in the kitchen, the cupboard by the door, on the top shelf."

And another, equally unbelievable, equally calm. "I've got a couple of torches in my bedroom. I'll get them. I don't think your father's seriously burned . . . We got the flames out too quickly. Don't move. I'll have the torches in a second."

Hexham! He refused to accept the evidence of his ears. The voices were inside his head, not in the Red Man's room.

As Pip began to whimper, he moved down into the hall, peering through the smoke, the steam. Light came on in two cross-beams that intersected. What it revealed set loose a fury in him as violent as a convulsion. The Red Man who should have been dead, struggling and cursing, while Meg vainly tried to soothe him, and Hexham at the foot of the bed tearing away sodden, scorched sheets and blankets.

The smoke, the stench of burning, the ruin past all redemption of his life as far as he could see ahead made it a scene lifted straight out of hell.

Pip let out a scream, and Meg turned. "Ashley . . . oh, darling . . . Of all the dreadful things to happen, Daddy must have set his bed on fire. But Hexham was here . . . I don't know how or why, but thank God he was or the house would have been burned down. If only we had some proper lights . . ."

Under delayed shock, the clogging after-effect of sleeping pills that hadn't been potent enough to deafen her to a scream for help, her calm began to dissolve. She tottered towards him, grabbed Pip, and then leaned, breathing hard against a tall-boy for support.

Hexham, kneeling by the bed, raised his head to an angle where it was hit by the torch-beam. Still willing himself to believe that a fragment of hope had escaped extinction, Ashley found himself staring into eyes that reflected back at him his own undying hate, plus the tincture of some other emotion. He had not defined it when from the bed came the blast of a pistol firing, the reek of gunpowder. For perhaps two seconds they were all imprisoned in the silence of absolute shock, their mouths gaping stupidly, before Ashley, with the grace of an actor playing a part, slumped to the floor.

Chapter 13

In an atmosphere of damning silence Ross examined the haggard, determinedly aloof face three feet from his own. To sum up: an hour's grinding work, no visible profit. To cover frustration that would give support and comfort to his adversary, he said with a heavy attempt at humour: "The one commodity we're not short of, Mr Price, is time. Suppose we go through it once more. We'll start with the knife."

Richard flung a glance loaded with contempt round the office: four police officers of assorted grades posted at strategic points to register every inflexion in his voice, any expression, gesture revealing an overtone of guilt, chose sarcasm as his weapon. "I find this Gestapo method of the knock on the door at dawn on Sunday, being whisked away in a fast car, a quite ridiculous piece of melodrama. Decidedly outdated."

"Not dawn, Mr Price," Ross snapped back. "Seven A.M. We don't work by the clock. I could have knocked you up at one A.M. but I waited until a more reasonable hour. Now, if you don't mind, I'd like you to repeat your story of the knife."

"You've heard it twice. How many more times?"

"*Once* more. To help you, I'll recap. You purchased the

one I have here at approximately 5.30 yesterday evening from a jeweller, Montgomery & Sons, in Beach Street. What I want to know is why you did so, when you'd given me to understand in this office on Thursday morning that you already had a knife similar to the one I showed you then at home."

It winked brightly at him from Ross's desk, a toy fashioned out of an ounce of silver and mother of pearl, too insignificant to constitute a threat. He jerked his glance away, met the eyes, given different dimensions by the drooping lid, thought what an unattractive, even repellent face it was, before he spoke with a voice tuned to justifiable exasperation: "My daughter gave me such a knife as a Christmas present, either three or four years ago. On Thursday I was under the impression that it was in my desk at home. But when I checked, it wasn't. Yesterday I bought the one you've seen fit to confiscate from me as a replacement."

"But why? That's what I want to know."

"Because I thought it conceivable that you might describe the one you found in a press release, that my wife might read about it in a newspaper, remark on its similarity to the present Jinny gave me. And, childlike, she would promptly ask me to produce it." His smile was openly sceptical. "You probably wouldn't know, but small children retain a proprietary interest in the presents they give. Jinny would have been upset if I'd lost hers."

"I get *that* point, Mr Price, but not why it was imperative to purchase an exact duplicate of the one found in your former wife's grave. Surely a child's memory would not have been so precise. You visited four shops before you found the one you wanted."

"What a bore for your men tailing me!"

"They didn't. We merely informed every shop within a certain radius of your home with such articles for sale that we'd be obliged if they'd report to us if they sold a pocket-sized pearl-handled fruit knife to a customer answering to your description."

He leaned forward, went on in harsh, barely controlled anger: "Mr Price, if you won't tell me, I'll tell you. Until two years ago, you carried a small fruit-knife in your pocket, probably as a compliment to your little daughter. It dropped out on the afternoon you murdered Monica Price, got swept with the rest of the rubble into her grave. Either you didn't miss it—or you did and were confident it would never be found. On Thursday, when I showed it to you, you swore you'd not lost yours, that it was at home, so put yourself to the trouble of proving that it was. Trouble which you'd have saved yourself if you'd denied ever possessing such a knife. But that was a risk you daren't take. There was always the chance of someone remembering that, some while ago, you were in the habit of keeping it in your pocket. You may have showed it to friends, office colleagues, pressed them to admire it . . . Parents are notoriously proud of the gifts their children give them, Mr Price, even if, intrinsically, they aren't of much practical value."

The shaft of irony spent, he ordered: "Now we'll go back to the matter of the five pound note."

"A waste of time, surely! It wasn't mine."

"But it was, Mr Price. Returning from Helton on the thirtieth of May two years ago, you found yourself running short of petrol, pulled into Amberside Garage, outside Helton, asked for five gallons, handed the attendant what you presumably believed was a pound note, seven shillings in silver, told him to keep the change. It wasn't until he was putting the money in the till that he discovered what you'd given him was a five pound note. He ran after you, tried to attract your attention, but you were so engrossed in making a quick get-away, that you didn't see him. He was an honest lad; he guessed you'd discover your mistake, return to claim your money so he noted down the number of your car, passed it on to his boss when he went off-duty.

"A fortnight later when there'd been no claimant, the boss told him he could keep the change, with the proviso that if the customer did return, he'd have to refund it. He had in mind that the driver might be from a distance. But it was you, Mr Price, wasn't it? Better to lose three pounds thirteen shillings than call attention to the fact that you were on that particular road that particular evening."

Richard smiled disdainfully. "You've certainly kept busy! Questioning every garage, maybe every householder on the road between here and Helton! What comes next, an identity parade where a boy who only saw me for half a minute two years ago, puts a hand on my shoulder and swears: 'That's him, sir!'"

"We don't need to ask Bill Henderson to identify you, Mr Price. He noted down the number of the car. His boss entered it in the Day Book. It was the number of the car you owned at that time, the one you traded in on the sixth of April this year. That's all checked, Mr Price. You drove to Helton and back on the afternoon of May thirtieth, two years ago."

"Have you tested the boy's long-distance vision?"

"Naturally. It's perfect." Ross stretched out his hand, drew towards him the cellophaned scrap of paper, pivoted it towards Richard. "This sketch-map of the route between Brighton and Helton is undoubtedly a rough copy of the one Monica Price sent you as a guide to Keeper's Cottage."

"Let *me* recap this time, Superintendent. I told you half an hour ago that I never received such a route from her. Why should I? I had no use for one."

Ross turned it over, held the underside towards Richard. "On the back she scribbled two sets of initials. D.D. and H.R.H. Two separate times neither of which, unfortunately, is legible. One of those initials is yours, Mr Price, evidence that she expected you to meet her at Keeper's Cottage. Which?"

Richard sighed elaborately. "Neither. You should know my name by now: Richard Edward Price."

"Oh, we do. Let's take the D's first. One might stand for Dick, don't you think, a common diminutive of Richard?"

"I have never been addressed as Dick."

"Not in any circumstances! I wonder. Though she appears to have had no high regard for you as a husband, when you fell in love with another woman, Monica Price became both resentful and possessive, didn't she? Probably threatened to make life very uncomfortable for you, sue you for desertion if you set up house with Sylvia Markham! Even when the present Mrs Price became pregnant, she refused you a divorce until she'd stripped you of everything you had: bank balance, car, home, furniture. Some while later, probably shortly before she was murdered, she must have discovered to her surprise that fortune had smiled on you, that you had achieved a higher living standard than she enjoyed. That must have maddened her, reminded her of an old nickname that wasn't very flattering. I'm going to suggest that she called you Dirty Dick. D.D. I'm correct, aren't I?"

"No."

Imperceptibly Ross's facial muscles relaxed, suggesting he'd caught a faint, hardly discernible note of desperation in the denial. "All right, Mr Price. We'll go through it once more. This time we'll go back to that Sunday morning. Now, it is established fact that the present Mrs Price and your daughter were absent from home that particular weekend in May two years ago. You were, presumably, somewhat anxious about Mrs Harris's health, how your wife would manage to cope with a sick mother and a small child. You must have wished that you'd been able to accompany her, ease her burden. But that wasn't possible, was it . . . because you had a date with Monica at Keeper's Cottage, in Dene Valley, Helton. Now, let's start from the moment you woke up that morning, go on from there."

To have cheated death by a hair's breadth, not once, but twice, had raised Frederick Gasson's morale to a peak of calm beyond the reach of his lashing temper. For the first time since his daughter's marriage, he was reinstated as supreme master in his own house, and Mr Ashley Jones had vindicated every charge he'd ever laid against him, sunk himself past redemption. Examining his burnt fingers, scorched right arm bandaged by Dr Pratt, he thought with awe: "By golly, I'm indestructible."

There was a new mattress under him, the bed-linen was fresh, but he'd resisted all efforts to move him into a different room. He wanted to feast his eyes on the smoke-stained walls, the black holes in the carpet, the scorched wood . . . evidence of attempted murder that must be preserved intact for police examination.

When Meg looked in at 9.30, he asked in the reasonable tone of one requesting a small service due to him: "Get on the phone to Helton Police, tell whoever answers that I want to see Superintendent Ross. They needn't bother with sending anyone else. It's him I want. And this morning."

Meg reminded herself of the terrifying shock to which he'd subjected himself, the minor injuries he'd sustained, before she answered in a kind but adamant tone: "No, Daddy. I'm not going to call the police, and neither are you."

Without deigning to reply, he pressed his bell, and when Hexham appeared, ordered: "Hexham, get me . . ."

Meg interrupted. "Daddy, listen to me, please wait . . ."

"Wait," he mocked savagely, "for what? Until he has another go at burning me alive in my own bed!"

"Daddy," she said despairingly, "must you! Couldn't you, just for once, behave like a normal man, face up to facts. What happened to you last night is that you fell asleep while you were smoking. I'm as much to blame for the fire as you are. When I got home I should have checked that you hadn't got any matches by you. I didn't, and I find it hard to forgive myself."

There was such a horrible grin of disbelief on his face, that she turned her glance from it, was compelled to draw a deep breath to gain control over nearly ungovernable rage. "It's absolutely monstrous what you're saying that Ashley deliberately started the fire. If anyone calls the police it should be him." She pointed accusingly to the shattered door frame. "You fired that old gun of Sam Goodsell's you inveigled him into loading for you, right at Ashley. Ashley didn't try to murder you, you tried to murder him!"

"But I didn't, did I? All I did was to nick him behind the ear, stun him for ten minutes. I'm not denying I fired at him. I'll 'confess,' don't you worry. Any man in my place would have been justified in firing a gun at him after he'd seen him creeping out of the room, leaving me in a blazing bed, walking off, going upstairs cool as you please while I fried to death!"

She said, straining for a last remnant of calm: "You imagined you saw Ashley. Or maybe you dreamed it. BUT IT DID NOT HAPPEN. Ashley wasn't near your room, not even downstairs. He woke up when you began screaming, went out on to the landing, saw the fire, and went back to grab Pip. What else would you have expected him to do?

The fire might have spread upstairs. And it would too—she turned her head—"if a friend of Hexham's mother's hadn't arrived unexpectedly on Saturday evening, so there wasn't a bed for him. You owe him your life . . ."

"No," Hexham countered quickly. "Mrs Jones, please."

"It's the truth. I'd like to think my father had remembered to thank you . . ."

"I wouldn't have had to," Frederick replied, "if that husband of yours wasn't a devil incarnate who sees nothing wrong in building a fire under the bed of a paralysed man, after he's fused the lights."

"Lights! You know perfectly well they've fused of their own accord twice in the last year." She glared at him, hoping the dementia that had got hold of him, would show signs of burning out. The vainness of the hope destroyed her self-control past recall, and she shouted: "If you get Superintendent Ross here, accuse Ashley of trying to murder you, when it was you who went berserk, fired a gun at him, I'll . . ."

"Well, go on," Frederick prompted when she stopped in mid-sentence. "Don't lose your nerve, girl. If I get Ross here, what will you do? I've a right to know."

"We'll leave you." She stated the fact with a degree of cool indifference that suggested the decision had been made without the least equivocation. "The three of us will walk out of this house and never come back to it. Or you."

He let out a bellow of laughter. "You think he'd let you. You honestly believe he would take on a penniless wife and child, provide for you?" When she didn't answer, but stared at him with the cool dislike she might have given a stranger, the old, never extinct, volcano exploded inside him. "You'd starve. Not that there's any danger of that. He'll not budge out of this house until he's bundled out by the police."

She said so distantly that she hardly seemed involved: "If you telephone the police, Pip and Ashley and I will leave you. The choice is yours not mine."

For a long moment their eyes locked in a pitiless challenge, then Frederick altered the angle of his head, so that he was looking beyond her, at Hexham. "Get on the phone at once and tell Superintendent Ross to come here on the double. I want to report a case of attempted murder."

Almost casually Meg walked out of the room, went upstairs.

Ashley lay in bed, reading a newspaper. She touched the strip of sticking plaster behind his ear. "Darling, how are you feeling now? Does your head still ache?"

"Um, but it's better than it was."

Her smile of loving concern was suddenly washed out by the tears that burst from her eyes, spilled down her cheeks, a torrent over which she had no control.

Ashley's reaction was both exasperated and resigned. "Now what? Don't tell me another chapter of melodrama is about to unfold!"

Meg smeared her cheeks dry with her hands. "Daddy's telephoning the police, ordering Superintendent Ross to his bedside so that he can accuse you of trying to murder him."

Ashley touched the strip of sticking plaster, murmured: "Dr Pratt confiscated the pistol, but there are two witnesses, you and Hexham, to testify that he blasted it off at me."

"I'm not worried that anyone is likely to believe him! Of course, they wouldn't. But the fuss, the beastliness of it getting out, ugly, garbled." She shook her head in distress. "That's horrible enough, but what I won't stand is the unspeakable, inhuman way he's behaving to you, hating you as much as if what he's accusing you of were true. Hypnotising himself into believing it is. At this very moment he's lying downstairs deluding himself that when Ross comes he's going to put you in handcuffs, drive you off to prison. He's not in a rage about it, not even angry. He's enjoying himself! That's the unforgivable part."

She walked to the window, stood looking out in silence for so long, that he prompted: "So?"

"It's the end." When she turned round her face was so set in calm resolution it seemed impossible that a few minutes before it had been distorted by tears. "I've made allowances, as many as any human being can be expected to make, for how he is, the hell it must be for him, but I can't any more. I'm finished. I don't even wish I could forgive him."

Her smile was made peaceful almost happy by the steadfastness of her resolve. "I never thought I could bear to leave him; for one thing the mechanics would be too complicated. But downstairs, when I saw how absolutely merciless he was towards you, they worked themselves out. Nothing could be simpler. He'll need two male nurses instead of one. Then he'll never be left alone. A woman will have to come in to cook and clean. I'll soon find one, fix up a new routine with Dr Pratt. With luck, it should all be settled by the end of the week, and we'll be free to move out."

"Where?" he enquired softly.

"Darling, as if that mattered! Anywhere. A flat, furnished rooms. I've got nearly a hundred pounds in my current account. With what you have, it'll see us through until you get a job. I don't care how we live . . . but never, never again am I going to touch a penny of his charity."

He said in a voice of reason: "But you're all he's got, you and Pip. You're furious with him, and I don't blame you, but later, won't you come round to remembering that he's a sick, helpless old man, not entirely responsible for his actions?"

She said with spirit: "He's responsible all right. He knows perfectly well what he's trying to do, ruin you. I warned him, but he went ahead. That's all there is to it. We go!"

She came back to the bedside, dropped a kiss on his cheek. "Darling, don't you see what it means? You're free of a job you loathed, of being bossed around by him. Doesn't that make you happy?"

"Yes." He smiled tranquilly at her. "Of course it does, but I wouldn't want you to suffer . . ."

"I shan't," she said gaily. "Once I've made my mind up, I never re-make it. I promise you, I won't have a single regret . . . ever."

When he was alone, the hot anguish of disappointment at seeing cherished dreams reduced to dust, which had possessed him outside the Red Man's room in the early hours of the morning, swung back, its ferocity doubled. Meg! No longer a loving, compliant ally, but transformed into his most invincible enemy.

So take stock, sum up. Even now, was the situation irretrievable? Would Meg's obstinacy withstand the cold blast of pauperism? Wouldn't the sight of Pip in need bend her pride, send her begging to her father? And wouldn't abject loneliness, the call of blood, force the Red Man's hand out in welcome? Given time, it was a predictable enough ending, but out of the last so-precious stretch of his youth he'd no time to spare pandering to their obduracy.

Savagely he flung himself out of bed, stood upright, hate so virulent that it provided a new source of strength. Dimly, beyond catastrophe he became aware of new horizons beckoning him . . . a star of deliverance. In response his spirits zoomed, became brilliantly light. Three words: Cut his losses. A wrench of pain, admittedly, at so much effort spent to so little profit, but it was a pain that would be healed by the balm of freedom.

He had to act quickly, be away before Ross arrived, also take with him no single article to suggest flight. No jacket on a day that was overhot for wearing one around house and garden; no article that would cause a pocket to bulge suspiciously. In the end he was forced to limit himself to a diamond-studded watch that had been the Red Man's gift to Meg on her twenty-first birthday; odds and ends of antique jewellery she'd inherited from her mother.

In the downstairs hall Meg and Hexham were in a huddle. Meg seeing him, ran towards him with breathless concern. "Darling, are you quite sure you're fit enough to be up?"

"I'm fine, except that I'm badly in need of fresh air. That bedroom's like an oven."

Hexham said: "Mr Gasson asked me to let you know that Superintendent Ross hopes to be here about mid-day."

Ashley laughed tolerantly. "And Mr Gasson would like me to hold myself available for questioning!"

Meg said firmly: "I would, too, darling. Since Ross is coming, he's got to know about Daddy firing the pistol at you. I've phoned Dr Pratt. He's promised to be here."

"Don't worry. I'll be on hand. I'm only going to do my usual Sunday morning chores on the car."

Meg laid a restraining hand on his arm. "But should you? Won't bending make your headache worse?"

He eased himself free of her grasp. "Topping up the batteries, checking the petrol and oil!"

"All right. But take care. Promise me you will?"

"I'll take care."

He left an interval of five minutes before he started the car. No use deluding himself that Meg and Hexham wouldn't hear it, burst out of the house to demand where he was going. If either or both appeared, he intended to keep his foot down, yell that he'd run out of petrol, would be back in no time at all. But when he turned out of the drive there was no sign of Meg's blue skirt, Hexham's white coat. Maybe his guardian angel, after a spell asleep, was on duty again, had arranged for Hexham to be tied to one of his obscene nursing duties, prodded Pip to let out an urgent howl for Meg.

Now that his only obstacle was a race against time, he was as wildly exhilarated as if he'd been watching a roulette wheel spinning, sure his number was coming up.

Three minutes to reach the showroom, not much more to rifle the deed box of passport and cash, cram them into his trouser pockets. And then into the car, the escape hatch open, the weekday evening dream transformed into solid, breathing reality.

Calculating there was a marginal risk that his absence from Laburnum Lodge might lend sufficient credibility to the Red Man's accusation to persuade Ross to mount police checks on the Channel and air ports, he'd decided to make for the air ferry to Le Touquet, a mere forty minutes' hard driving away. Say Ross arrived about noon. Ten minutes listening to the Red Man, plus a further ten while Meg laughed him to scorn, added her own contribution about the pistol . . . there was an even chance that he'd be on French soil before Ross's orders were put into action.

Air ferry planes invariably had odd spare seats left empty by passengers travelling two or even one to a car. Ditching the Jaguar . . . that hurt damnably. But without A.A. documents and a reservation he hadn't a hope of getting transport across the Channel in the holiday season. It was a deprivation that cut so deep he had instantly to promise himself that by some means before nightfall he'd have equipped himself with another.

Crumley was behind him, a write-off. He'd never set eyes again on the Red Man, or Meg; never have to meet Ross's mean, ferret gaze. Monica was consigned to limbo. H.R.H.

The bitch. In his head he heard her voice sneering: His Royal Highness. When she'd first used it, teasingly, dotingly, he found it flattering, but not later when it turned to a derisive taunt. She must have written it down somewhere . . . how else could Ross have got hold of it? Well, damn her to hell for all eternity . . . he was through with beating his brains out wondering who'd murdered her.

At the moment when he was banishing the thought for ever, he was checked by an explosion of excitement. He pulled it back, re-examined it. If he was able to assure himself that he didn't care who'd killed Monica, it meant that, for the first time he was certain past a doubt that he hadn't! And he was, absolutely certain. Why? What was the positive factor that made him sure?

Before he could find it, he was struck into a frenzy of alarm at the sight of Prince emerging at a fast lope from the entrance to Beechgrove Farm.

What the hell was Ian doing allowing him loose on a main road, at the mercy of unrestricted traffic! He honked, and for a second Prince havered, then continued to drift towards the crown of the road. The choice was clean-cut: drive on and mow him down, or swerve dangerously. Imagination provided a fore-vision of the mangled, blooded body, and the decision made itself.

As the car left the road, and he rode the air, his mind attained such a superhuman degree of lucidity that the solution of the most intricate problem was reduced to a process of elementary arithmetic, like adding two and two together. In that unearthly state the question he'd asked himself a moment before answered itself. He hadn't murdered Monica because the flesh on the body he'd handled had been clay-cold, the hair a stiff mat of drying blood.

He'd remembered! Which meant that he'd subdued and mastered the minute fracture in his brain cells, willed the dead tissues of memory to yield back to him the minutes they'd stolen, buried away in darkness.

Victory over his last enemy! At the moment of impact he was shouting aloud: "Glory hallelujah!"

Chapter 14

With the inquest, funeral over, not even the stark finality of death was powerful enough to cancel out the household routine: there was Pip to be fed, all his vociferous demands to be met, meals to be provided for her father and Hexham. Meg took up her domestic duties with a stoicism that wore the outward skin of near-serenity. The only visible crack was that she could not endure Pip out of her sight. For every moment of the day he had to be within reach of her outstretched hand: proof that half her world had survived catastrophe.

It was past mid-day, Pip's lunch ready to spoon into him as soon as she'd got him into his high chair, when Hexham entered the kitchen, said so quietly it sounded like an apology: "Mrs Jones, Superintendent Ross is waiting in the hall, asking if he may see you."

"No." Her refusal was so iron firm that, when he did not immediately turn to take it back to Ross, she added an explanatory footnote for him. "I don't have to talk to any more policemen . . . ever."

"You don't have to, but he's making rather an issue of it. I asked him what it was about. He said he needs your help."

She blazed into indignation: "My help!"

He said soothingly: "I don't think it has anything to do with the accident. It's something else."

The accident, the scent of which lay about her like an evil-smelling miasma, despoiling the air she breathed. The accident that had struck Ashley dead at the moment in time when he was abandoning his wife and son, his pockets stuffed with jewellery he'd stolen from her, a passport he had applied for before their marriage was a month old, a cache of money he'd hoarded against a need to make an instant escape from her . . . No, not from her, from her father.

"Then what?" she demanded shortly.

Ross's bulk eased through the door. Meg wheeled on him, spoke with the bluntness of one issuing an order. "Superintendent, this is my kitchen. You have no right to enter it without being invited to do so by me."

He half dipped his head. "I have no right. But I hope when I have explained why I am here, you will forgive my intrusion. I give you my word that I won't stay a moment longer than necessary."

With open reluctance she gave Hexham a signal of dismissal.

She did not ask Ross to sit down; he did not appear to expect it. He took an envelope from his pocket, extracted four cards, which he laid out on the table. "When your husband died, Mrs Jones, these were found in his wallet. Would you be good enough to read them."

She did so, then lifted her gaze to his, said uncaringly: "What are they, part of some stupid game?"

"They were written by a man or a woman who had some knowledge of your late husband's friendship with Monica Price. All of them were posted in Crumley between the date when her body was found and the Friday before your husband was killed. There is no actual attempt at extortion but the inference is plainly there. The writer believed, or purported to believe, that your husband had a hand in Monica Price's murder."

"Then," she said indifferently, "whoever wrote the cards was wrong. Since you've arrested Richard Price, you're in the best position to know how wrong! So why come bothering me with stupid questions?"

"Monica Price's divorced husband hasn't yet been brought to trial. A jury could acquit him of her murder."

She burst out: "Oh, for heaven's sake, come to the point. What are you trying to say?"

"Mrs Jones, the police do not arrest a suspect, charge him with murder unless they possess sound evidence that he is guilty. We believe Richard Price murdered Monica Price. We know she was blackmailing him. They met at Keeper's Cottage on the Sunday afternoon she was killed. He was to bring with him a sum of £1,000. When it came to the crunch he had been unable to raise more than £250. He begged her for an extension of time to pay. She wouldn't give it to him. The outcome was a violent quarrel, some sort of fight, in which, either intentionally or by accident, he killed her. This is not surmise but facts that Richard Price has freely confessed.

"But he maintains that he did not bury her, nor touch her car. We are inclined to believe him. When he found she was dead, he panicked, drove away. Later, presumably having collected himself sufficiently to reason that he had a better chance of escaping the penalty for either murder or manslaughter if he hid the body, he returned, intending to do so. But he couldn't find it; only a mound of rocks and stones below which someone, in the interval of the couple of hours he had spent driving around, had done the job for him, also taken away and sunk her car in the pond from which we recovered it. We believe that someone was your husband."

She gave a hoot of derision. "Surmise with a vengeance! My husband never went near Keeper's Cottage. Why should he?"

"We know that Monica Price urgently required not the £1,000 she was trying to extort from her former husband, but £2,000. So it becomes logical to assume that she was blackmailing two men: Richard Price and someone else. At the time in question your husband was . . . well, shall we say vulnerable. We think he was her second victim. She could have arranged to meet him in the same place, later on the same day. When, with or without the £1,000, he arrived at Keeper's Cottage, it was to discover that she'd been murdered."

She said scathingly: "Leaving aside the rest of your fairy-tales about my husband being vulnerable to blackmail, which he was not, why should he go to the trouble of bury-ing a woman he hadn't murdered?"

"Maybe because he was jittery in case he should find him-self under suspicion of murdering her. Or because he had reason to be thankful she was dead, and was anxious to hide her car, get her body into a grave that was unlikely to be discovered once the reservoir was flooded."

"You're playing a guessing game," she said sweetly, and then anger broke in her and she shouted: "Prove what you say! You can't because you haven't any proof. Go on, admit it, you've got no proof."

"No absolute proof," he said quietly, "but we have to re-member that your husband was fleeing the country when he was killed."

"Because," she said with acid distinctness, "my father had, the night before, tried to murder him. You must remember that too, Superintendent. So please take your silly cards away; I can't think why you brought them here."

"Because we are convinced that whoever wrote them knew something we don't; may even have seen your husband near Keeper's Cottage that Sunday afternoon."

"Then why wait two years to say so?"

"It was two years before we discovered Monica Price's body. Until it was unearthed, the writer may not have known it was buried in Keeper's Cottage, even that a murder had been committed there." He looked directly into her coldly sardonic glance, bitterly resentful at being left with no course but to go on begging. "Mrs Jones, have you any idea who wrote these cards to your husband?"

"None."

"He never mentioned them, showed them to you?"

"No. For the very last time, Superintendent, my husband had not the remotest connection with that woman's murder. He neither killed her nor buried her. Is that all?"

"No. There is one more question I have to ask you. It is an important one. Have you ever, in any connection, heard the initials H.R.H. applied to your husband? Did he ever assume a name for which they might stand? Did you ever hear him addressed by a nickname with those initials?"

"No, never. He was christened Ashley Jones. He never *assumed* any other name. Why should he! He wasn't a criminal." She bent, lifted Pip out of his play-pen. "And now, I must really ask you to excuse me."

He gathered up the cards slowly, fingers made clumsy by burning disappointment. Half-way he stopped, made a final plea: "Mrs Jones, if it would help you to identify the writer I can tell you that there is a woman's fingerprint on three of the cards."

"It doesn't."

He said with hot condemnation: "You're not interested

188

in identifying a mischief-making poison-pen, not interested in the possibility of clearing your dead husband's name?"

She held Pip close, spoke disdainfully over his head. "My husband's name does not need clearing, Superintendent, except in your records, which are of no interest to anyone but you. I couldn't care less who wrote those silly cards. If you want to take them seriously, that's your affair, not mine. Good day, Superintendent. If you wouldn't mind showing yourself out."

When he'd gone, she fed Pip, spooning the food into his mouth that sometimes opened and sometimes stayed mulishly shut until she made a joke that distracted him into accepting the spoon: engrossed wholly in him, yet the eyes of her mind absorbed in re-reading the lines of block letters, every word of which she remembered. A woman! For once, Ross had guessed right.

Herself and Libby Soames, moved up from kindergarten into the big school at Helton, sharing a double desk, labouring over their exercise books. In those days Helton High School for Girls taught its younger pupils to print before they were allowed to join their letters. Odd, how the knack stayed with you. For instance, when she wrote a label for a parcel she automatically slid back into print. There'd been a certain style to their block capitals that made them instantly identifiable to anyone who'd learnt to shape them under the same teacher.

Libby, she thought, emotions drained to a depth where she was incapable of astonishment or curiosity. Libby, knowing nothing, because there was nothing for her to know, but lashing out, wildly guessing, giving vent to a spiteful urge to tease that Meg, no one better knew, was endemic in her nature. Spitting mischievous little barbs at Ashley because he'd not been blinded by her looks into marrying her. A week ago, and she'd have sped, outraged, to castigate, condemn. Not now. Ashley no longer needed her to defend his innocence. He was safe. Secure for ever from Libby, her father, from Ross, even from the wretched Monica Price. Ashley was safe.

When Meg paid a duty visit to her father's room, Frederick Gasson looked beseechingly into his daughter's face, his most desperate need, an absolution for which he dared not apply. By rights he should have been a happy man, but he'd been cruelly cheated of his rights. Meg hated him. If only she had broken down, raved at him, he might have found a way to crack the wall of ice behind which she had barricaded herself against him. But she never showed a sign of doing so.

Setting Pip down to crawl about his favourite play-haunt, under his grandfather's bed, she enquired if he had all he needed.

The question was too perfunctory and uncaring to require an answer. Instead he asked: "How are you? That's what I want to know."

"I'm all right."

A cool breeze, the first one for weeks, was flowing into the room. As she crossed to the window, to protect him from the cross-current of air he disliked, he stared at her helplessly, wanting to shout that she'd been spared a lifetime of misery, deceit, couldn't she even admit that! But not daring to. Instead he heard himself saying weakly: "You were twelve when your mother died. You won't remember much about it. But I do. That's why I know how you're feeling now."

"Do you," she said so absently, that it was plain to him she hadn't taken in what he'd said. She'd go to her grave mourning a man who'd married her for her money and when he'd wrecked all chances of ever getting his hands on it, deserted her. Were all women condemned to be fools?

Turning from the window, for the first time since she'd left him on that Sunday morning at the moment when Hexham was picking up the telephone, she allowed her glance to focus on his person. She looked for a long time in silence, while he gazed into a face that had, amazingly, changed little in the last week. Except her eyes, he thought. They were no longer the eyes of a girl.

"Meg?" he whispered.

She sighed. "What you're saying is that other women lose their husbands, survive. That I shall. But I don't need telling."

She lifted her head, so that her gaze was no longer on him, but beyond in a mid-distance he couldn't see. Immense dignity came to her, even a kind of pride, as she reached deeply for a truth and spoke it aloud. "I always knew I wouldn't keep him for ever. I don't know how I knew, but I did."

He said gruffly: "Loving someone is a punishing business. Parts of it are hell."

"In my case," she said quietly, "the hell comes when it is over."